The Things Lily Knew

THE FOURTH IN A SERIES

SHERRY BOAS

Caritas Press, Arizona, USA

THE THINGS LILY KNEW

Sherry Boas

First Edition

10 9 8 7 6 5 4 3 2 1

978-0-9833866-7-4

Published by Caritas Press, Arizona, USA

For reorders and other works by Sherry Boas, visit www.LilyTrilogy.com.

For my mom and dad, who were the first to show me what love is.

Contents

1

The Proposal

I used to love the clouds. I made it a point to know all of their names. Cirrus, Stratus, Cumulonimbus. I admired them not for their potential to produce, but for pure aesthetics — their beauty and their physical character and their ability to change a plain dull sky into a masterpiece of shapes and textures. But now, I resent their sublimity, floating beneath me on a pale blue sky. How dare they flaunt their beauty? How dare they try to deceive anyone — particularly me — into believing there is anything but ugliness in this world?

The moon is in on it too, for some reason, and I feel the same disgust for it. Why is it out this time of day? Small and distant, calling my thoughts outward to itself, having me believe in things that are not.

A jolt wakes the passenger in the aisle seat and he clears his throat vigorously as the sound of creaking plastic reminds me we are all at the mercy of physics and flight mechanics and inner-ear equilibrium, all combining to determine how well our digestive system can withstand the "potholes in the sky," as Frank used to describe them to Lily. I suppose I could see the turbulence as a metaphor, but I am too tired and too spent for metaphors.

I think about calling my cousin John. Sometimes when I've had a rough day, I call him and beg him to tell me that something makes sense in this insane world. Nine times out of ten he fulfills my request with a selection from his vast

1

repertoire of Lily. But I know that on a day like today, not even John will bring me any peace. This loss is too big, although I am not so devoid of hope that I can discount the possibility that the thought of Lily, unlike the beauty of clouds, might someday make me smile again.

That would be my Aunt Lily, my father's little sister, John's aunt and childhood playmate, entertainer, advocate, protector and comforter.

I have felt a connection to her ever since I read Beverly Greeley's account of her life with Lily. I do not exaggerate when I say that if Lily had not existed, neither would I have been born. Because of Grandma Bev's honest and, at times, harrowing appraisal of life with Lily, my mother decided to carry me, accepting the fact I would be born with Down syndrome and accepting all that goes with it — the good, the bad, the ugly and the beautiful.

I was not born with Down syndrome. Sometimes I wish I had been. But no. I was born with an exceptional intellect. I say this in all honesty and without conceit. It just is the way it is, and I had nothing to do with it. It is pure gift, and I take no credit. But I live inside it. Like a child lives inside her father's house and is even given her own room, but has done nothing to merit or earn it, that is how I live. I am quite happy with all the many gifts that I have been provided because it makes life much easier on many levels. But there is a lot to take care of. There are many valuables and many things I must guard against getting broken or weathered by the elements. There are things that must be updated and upgraded, lest they become obsolete. Then there's the formidable task of dusting. If it were a simpler space, I think I should not be any less happy. Some of the happiest people I have known have simplicity — in their intellect and in their understanding.

I have always had a brain that could grasp things about eight times faster than most of my friends could. And one that would obsess over finding answers to questions that no one else would even think of asking. Once, when I was a very small

2

child, I spent nearly two hours in deep thought about this question: How does one throw away the trash can?

Aunt Lily had an inferior brain, and she could have answered the question in about twenty seconds. Don't ask me what she would have come up with. I still haven't figured it out.

I'm now approaching my 30s, and as I said, a very smart woman, and answers elude me now more than ever. I originally came on this trip hoping to find the answer to a much more difficult question than that of the trash can. But now I am engulfed in the amoebic endoplasm of grief, and that very pressing question whose answer will govern the rest of my life, not to mention the future of life on this planet, will have to wait. At the moment, I care not one bit about finding the answer to any question. Except this one: Why?

Not why did it happen. Tragedy happens all the time in all corners of the universe, and I've never known anyone who found it useful to ask why. But I'd like to know the reason my love was not strong enough to prevent it. I could have tried to save him, but I froze. And he was in harm's way only because of me. What was the purpose of our paths crossing?

I wish I could have that day back — the day when I met Marty. I would not have reached out my hand to accept his card. I really had no business entering his world. I had a world of my own, and that day, it was breaking open before me quite nicely:

The sun strands pushed their way through the leaves, flitting and landing like illuminated moths on the tree-lined highway. The dedication of the new facility for the mentally and physically disabled would be attended by a huge cross-section of humanity — mayors and architects and attorneys as well as busboys, grocery baggers and custodians. Logan, a brilliant man I've been seeing for eight months, was to give a speech, which he recited under his breath as he drove.

"I still can't figure out why they put this place so far out, in the middle of nowhere," I said, watching the trees whiz by.

He held a finger up at me as he continued his under-breath recitation, squinting at the road.

"Seems like many of the people it is intended to serve won't be able to access it way out here," I continued.

He held up the same finger and proceeded with his whispers.

I stared out the window, pretending to be interested in the passing trees, to alleviate the awkward reality of having been shushed — twice.

"OK," he said finally. "I think I've got it. I think I've nailed this speech."

He reached over and squeezed my hand. "The whole point of it is to give them a place away from it all. A place where they can listen to the brook babble past. You can understand that, can't you?" As if I needed to do some great thinking about this, as if this thought would tax my brain. He patted my hand and returned his to the steering wheel to navigate the winding road.

"Rhodes Scholars do not need to be patronized quite as much as the others you have the misfortune of having to interact with, my Dear," I said patting him on the knee in return. "I think I can stretch my understanding."

"I'm sorry, Love. I didn't mean that the way it sounded. Forgive my clumsiness."

"Of course."

"You know how I feel about your intelligence."

"Of course. You know I suffer no insecurities in that department."

"I think we are quite well matched. But there is one thing at which I doubt anyone could be your rival."

"And what is that one thing?"

"Sarcasm, my dear, You are the champ."

"Thank you. How sweet."

"Well, I regret that they didn't offer a program of study in sarcasm at Princeton, or I might well be able to keep up with you."

"Nor did they at Oxford, so I majored in genetics to have something to fall back on. Sarcasm is just a hobby, really, and I am self-taught."

He chuckled in his dignified way. "Anyway, the awards board did not seem at all dismayed by the location of the facility. So I will assume it is in the exact right place."

"It's just that it's such a nice facility, with so much to offer. I just think more people would be able to take advantage of all it offers if it were closer in."

"You aren't the first to feel that way and I'm sure you won't be the last. Nevertheless, there it stands." We pulled into a massive parking lot, where attendants in neon orange vests waved us through to the VIP parking. The huge three-story building is made mostly of windows, to take in the forest view. Logan is a gifted architect, there's no doubt about it. I pondered how a glass building could look so at home in the sticks, but it really did work somehow. Maybe the unpredictable angles of the building itself or the way it was oriented on the parcel, a bit askew, jutting back into the trees. "Just try to be happy for me, Darling. I consider this award quite an honor."

"I know you do, Logan. And I am happy for you. This is a great achievement."

He kissed me on the forehead, placed his hand on my knee and squeezed. "It means the world to me that you are here to share it with me."

"I wouldn't miss it for the world." I wished I truly felt that way. Logan is a decent man with a good heart and a wide array of accomplishments, but I would just as soon have been home in my fuzzy slippers reading Dostoyevsky or watching an episode of *The History of Science*. Still, I had the strange sense that I was meant to be there. For what reason, I did not know. And I certainly don't now.

It was a much larger crowd than I expected with a number of dignitaries, including the mayor, who has a brother with cerebral palsy and the county attorney, who uses a wheelchair. We made our way through the crowd, Logan shaking hands and introducing me as we went. We ended up at the bar, where a tall, shapely blonde wearing a skin-tight royal blue pencil skirt with matching fitted blazer was drawing a crowd, speaking with poise and conviction about something to do with disability rights, and next to her, with his hand rested lightly on her back, was Brad Beauchamp. I wondered if he had already spotted me earlier and if so, how much he'd been watching me. I felt a strange emotion, which I'm not quite sure how to describe. Some mix of embarrassment and thrill. He would soon learn, if he hadn't already, that I was there with Logan Horne. He would assume it was all so false. Despite the fact that Logan Horne is the man of many women's dreams, Brad Beauchamp would surmise that I must be desperate, that I still suffer from a broken heart and can't bear to be alone.

Fortunately, Brad didn't seem to notice me before we all took our seats for the program. But as Logan was introduced and stood to approach the podium, I felt Brad's eyes on me. I glanced at him, and we both smiled politely. Then, I did not look at him again, devoting my attention to Logan's speech, which began with all the reasons why this was the most fulfilling project he'd ever taken on.

"Some people have criticized this facility because it is too far out." He looked into the crowd when he spoke, glancing only occasionally at his notes. "Maybe those people don't understand the indomitability of the human heart. Maybe their lives have not presented them with the challenges necessary to teach them what people with disabilities know. Life is not easy. And it was never meant to be. When you encounter an obstacle, you don't turn back, you get the pole vault. People who love this place, who find value in the programs and friendships that will take form here, will not let a few extra miles stand in their way. People who will love this place are used to going the extra mile."

I felt Brad's eyes on me again, but I didn't dare look at him.

I stood up and made my way to the hors d'oeuvres, hoping Logan would notice that I have lost interest in the rest of his speech. He didn't.

Brad suddenly appeared to my left and picked up a small plastic plate and a toothpick with a tempura shrimp.

"If I were going to be honest, I would have to admit that I really don't like him very much right now," I considered telling Brad as we stood together by the crab-stuffed mushrooms. Instead, I muttered, "I'm one of those wimpy people he is dressing down right now."

"What?"

"Oh, nothing."

"I don't like my date very much either," he said.

"Then why are you with her?"

"I don't know. I guess because I can't be with the one I really want."

"And who might that be?"

"I'm looking right at her."

"More games, Brad?"

"Games?"

"You don't want me. You're just bored with her. Do something to spice it up and try to make something work for once in your life."

"Wow. OK. Now I remember why it didn't work out between you and me. You are brutal."

"No, I am tired. Tired of wasting time."

"So, why are you with him?"

"I'm not."

"You're not?"

"Starting now. No, I'm not."

"Poor guy. Look at him up there giving his speech like he's at the top of the world. And you are about to shake him off the ladder and send him crashing to the ground."

"I wouldn't do that to him tonight, Brad. I'm not as brutal as you think I am."

The speech continued: "And I would like to say, in closing, that I owe a great debt to all of those people in my life who have always believed in me. They are too numerous to name individually, but you know who you are."

Brad spoke softly in my ear, warming my hair with his moist breath. "Just don't wait too long. It gets harder and harder to find your way out. Like being caught in a strange forest after dark. On a moonless night."

"You are so weird."

Logan continued: "But, of course, I cannot neglect to mention by name one special person because I am especially indebted to her. Without her to share it with, none of this would mean anything. She is the love of my life, Annabel Greeley." His eyes found my empty chair and then scanned the back of the room.

"I told you it gets harder." Brad winked.

Logan's eyes found me at the refreshment table and his smile widened, accentuating the crow's feet I have always found so attractive. "And speaking of Annabel Greeley," Logan returned his gaze to the crowd, "if she will agree, I'd like to make her my wife."

A chorus of "awwww," sung in what seemed like three part harmony, went up from the crowd and people looked around for this Annabel Greeley, only to find her with a stuffed mushroom half in and half out of her mouth, standing next to a tall, muscular, former lover, who was contemplating ways of getting rid of "former."

"What do you say, Darling Anna? Will you have me as your husband?"

There was a time I would have jumped at this. I would have released a torrent of pent up tears, damned in by years of searching and longing. I would have been in awe at the sequence of events that would have led to a man like Logan Horne wanting to spend the rest of his life with me. I am actually guilty of a bit of hero worship. But now, standing next to Brad, I remembered. I remembered something that I couldn't, at the moment, forget. It was powerful and I missed it — the feeling I had whenever I was with Brad. I did not delude myself into believing I could have it back permanently. Too much had happened between us and too much had happened since him. Now, the question for me was, do I stand still or do I keep moving? But the more pressing question at that moment was "Where in the heck are the napkins?" because now three hundred people were staring at me, waiting for my reply to a marriage proposal, and all I could manage to think was that I must surely have some kind of food on my face. From the time I was a baby and all through my teen years, in every photo ever taken of me, I had food either stuffed in my mouth or smeared on the outside of it. There came a point when I became reluctant to eat in public and I remained so until I met Brad, who even while still a student, was always getting invited by some prominent geneticist to some important affair that invariably included dinner.

I casually wiped over my mouth and chin with my right hand and rubbed my hands together to disseminate the food particles. "Well, I, uh. Well. What an amazing proposal. What girl wouldn't be honored to be asked to be your wife, Logan? Sounds like we've got quite a bit of talking about the future to do."

A roaring applause went up.

"As a matter of fact, it might not take much talking at all, my Love. Just two short words: I do. We've got a judge here tonight, and all of our good friends. We can just save the postage for the wedding invitations and the cost of catering and tie the knot right now. If you're crazy enough, Miss Greeley, to have a gauche, good-for-nothing dope like me for your life's partner."

I sensed a veiled apology woven through that proposal and my heart softened. "I'm not sure I'm quite as crazy as you are, my love. I think it would be better to do some planning."

The crowd was silent.

"As you wish, Miss Greeley. I will marry you wherever your dreams take us."

Applause. Grand applause. Brad rolled his eyes and shook his head, while offering a half dozen half-hearted claps.

Logan finished off his time at the podium with a joke: "An architect, an engineer and a contractor walk into a bar..." I joined him back at his seat after the polite laughter. He kissed me on the cheek and put his arm around me, looking around to see who was watching.

"So much for creative marriage proposals," he smiled sheepishly.

"Not exactly the You Tube moment you were hoping for there, Honey. I'm sorry."

"I'm sorry to put you on the spot like that, Darling. Forgive me. I just wanted it to be memorable for you."

Several speakers droned on about various technical aspects of the building and how it would be used and I began to appreciate, by contrast, Logan's ability to engage an audience. There is a certain quiet charisma about him, some spark that would make him suitable for parts in movies where the characters carry ornate, heirloom daggers and wear woolen capes. He is tall and slim, with well-defined bones in his face, which could make him look severe and humorless were it not for an ever-present and amiable — but not overstated — smile. His dark hair is long enough to be combed into a slight side wave, perfectly complimenting an ample, yet well-trimmed mustache. If you saw him, you'd expect him to open his mouth and speak British English, but out flows his American dialect, refined enough for American English, a bit East Coast, but not sophisticated enough to fit his physical presence. He wears expensive sport coats and white, crisply ironed shirts with the top two bottoms left open. "If I ever get invited to the White House or the Vatican," he is fond of saying, "I will wear a tie." He is a little smug when he says it, but not without charm.

When it was all over, Logan and I made our way through the crowd, shaking hands. Then, I remembered I left my purse at my seat and went to go collect it, while Logan proceeded with small talk.

That moment — that purse. Why could it not have been hanging on my shoulder, where it always was? As I bent to retrieve it under the chair, Brad stole up close to me. "I've got something really exciting going down, Bel," he whispered. "I have a business proposition for you. A big one. "

"Business?"

"I'm right on the cusp of something monumental, Bel. I'd like to talk to you about joining me. Never before has our field offered as much promise as this. Call me tomorrow, Bel. You still have my number, don't you?"

"Yes, I have it."

Don't forget, Bel. Call me."

ജ✄രു

2

The Tuba Player

When she was a little girl, Lily was always amazed that the hair bow laid out with her clothes every morning invariably happened to match. She would point to the bow and exclaim, "pink!" and then point to a stripe in her shirt and proclaim, "pink!" Or whatever color her ensemble happened to be that day. It never occurred to her that her Auntie Bev had actually planned it that way. Lily just thought it was serendipity or something. The universe, for some mysterious reason, provides matching hair accessories, although it was never expected or demanded. It was always a surprise, and it always made her grateful. Lily managed to be grateful for the smallest things. Well, unless, of course, it was a small piece of pizza. Then she was mad. It had to be a big piece of pizza. Or two pieces of pizza. Two big pieces of pizza. Not two small pieces. Or even two medium sized pieces. And no matter how big the one piece or the two pieces were, there was always room for one more and always a cross word if there wasn't one more. Unless there was dessert. In that case, the limited quantity of pizza was excusable. Not commendable, mind you, but excusable.

Pizza was pretty much the only vegetable Lily would eat. I know nutritionists don't consider pizza a vegetable, but it was the closest Lily was going to come to enjoying one. So, the people who worried about Lily's health tried to take comfort in that thin layer of tomato sauce between the dough and the cheese.

I remember visiting Frank and Lily and opening their freezer to find nothing but a stack of eight frozen pizzas, a bag of Tater Tots and a bag of French fries. The fridge had four loaves of Wonder bread, three packages of individually wrapped American cheese slices, four bottles of orange juice, a jug of chocolate milk, a bottle of mustard and a jar of mayonnaise. I wondered why no one did a food intervention. Shouldn't their family members, doctors and therapists have, at an appointed time and day, descended upon their little guest house and forced broccoli into their fridge and lentils into their pantry? Everyone must have realized that, once a person reaches a certain age, no matter if they have a disability or not, they will eat what tastes good and not what they would tell their children to eat.

I'm trying to remember now, why I was thinking about frozen pizza and Frank and Lily. Oh yes. The serendipity of the universe. The universe that provides color-matched hair bows. I was trying to determine if there was some opposite force to serendipity. One that makes bad things happen by sheer chance. If there is such a thing, it occurred at that moment when I went back to grab my purse at the dedication of the facility for the disabled. That was the moment when Brad delayed me with his pleas to call him about his business proposition and a group of people, all with different disabilities came toward us, led by a young man with a compact muscular build, tightly packed into a Bob Marley T-shirt. He had one arm around a woman with Down syndrome and a hand resting on the shoulder of a short middle aged man gripping a crutch and hobbling on different-length legs. A woman in a wheelchair with a withered arm looked into my face and smiled stiffly. "Hey, are you going to marry him?"

"Who? Him?" I asked pointing my thumb at Brad.

"No, the cute guy who wants you to marry him."

"I don't know," I shrugged

"You should marry him," said one round-faced woman with ruddy skin and thin blonde hair. "He's cute."

"You think so?" I asked.

"Yeah," she nodded emphatically. "If you don't want him, can I have him?"

"Maybe we shouldn't plan his life out for him without checking with him first, huh Marci?" said the muscular man, whose group home staff ID, suspended from a lanyard around his neck, identified him as "Marty." "Besides, I thought you wanted to marry me."

"That was before I saw Mr. Logan. No offense, Mr. Marty, but he sounds rich. And smart."

"Actually," I said to the woman, "the heart is more important than the brain or the wallet."

"Oh Mr. Logan has heart," she informed. "Look what he's done for us. This place is incredible."

"I like the elliptical trainer," said a man with Down syndrome, pushing up his sleeve and flexing his bicep. "Makes my muscles really big."

"I like the dance class," said the woman with Down syndrome. "I'm a good dancer."

I wondered if the two were a couple or if they ever would be. Or maybe they once were and broke up. Then I thought of Lily and Frank, and that suddenly seemed impossible. Frank and Lily had their share of spats, but breaking up would have been out of the question. I doubt it would have ever crossed their minds. At least not for more than a half hour.

Although, there was the one time Lily showed up at the main house with her little florescent pink suitcase. John was the only one home. "I coming to live with you," she informed him.

"Why? What happened?"

"They all babies." Calling someone a baby was the worst it could get. The ultimate insult.

John hugged her and took her inside. "Here, you sit down and I'll get you some Oreos. And you can tell me all about it."

"Frank is a baby," she proclaimed as she dropped her bottom onto the middle cushion of the sofa.

"How come?"

"He tell me I buy the wrong toilet paper. I buyed the one

with the yellow puppy. He clog the toilet. He use too much. He tell me buy 1,000. But I want the yellow puppy toilet paper. He say it my fault cuz I buy fat toilet paper. His poop is fat. That not my fault." She plunged a cookie into her milk and held it there. "And Frank's Mommy is a baby too."

"Why is Vera a baby?" John asked.

"She tell me I have to buy 1,000. I don' like 1,000. I like the puppy toilet paper."

"Maybe you'll need to make a little sacrifice, Aunt Lily. For the sake of your marriage. You don't want to find yourself in divorce court over something you wipe your butt on."

A smile grew broad across her face. It was the word "butt." A guaranteed laugh. Unless she was really mad. In that case, a guaranteed smile.

"I buy the soap he want. Why can' I have the puppy toilet paper? He wan' that soap that smell like pears. I don' like it. But I buy it. I like the one that smell like cherry almonds."

"Because it's pink."

"And it smell like cherry almonds."

"Guys don't like that."

"Frank like cherries. And Frank like almonds."

"Yes, to eat. Not to wash in."

"Well I don' like pears."

"I know what you want. You want pepperoni pizza scented soap."

"That would be weird."

"So is a married couple fighting over toilet paper and soap."

"We don' fight over soap. Jus' toilet paper and barbecue sauce."

"Barbecue sauce too?"

"Because he like Mr. Nibbs. But I like Sweet Baby Kay. He only like Mr. Nibbs because it got a picture of Mr. Nibbs. But it taste like Salami."

"Do you two ever fight over anything important? Like money?"

"No, we don' figh- abou- money. We both like money. The hundred is our favorite."

"Yeah. Mine too. Listen, Aunt Lily, why don't you go home and cook Frank a nice dinner?"

"Frank is a baby. I not cooking for a baby."

"Then give him Gerber's."

That broad smile returned, followed by a giggle and then a full blown belly laugh, which tipped her whole body to the side. John joined in and after a full thirty seconds, Lily managed to hoist herself off the couch, strength drained, but love renewed by laughter, picked up her suitcase, kissed John on the cheek and made her way to the door.

And so I imagine that true love always goes home. And I also imagine that people like Frank and Lily and the couple with Down syndrome that was standing before me that night possess a high propensity for true love. And I hate to say it, but I don't know that Brad or Logan or I do.

"So, you'll call me then?" Brad asked, placing his hand on my forearm. "I've got to run."

Brad's date was making her way toward us, with her very defined hips and almost non-existent waistline. She was walking with a middle-aged couple dressed in grey suits. They looked like attorneys to me. Probably met in law school. Probably a similar story to Brad's and mine. Up late studying together, planning to build a life together in their shared field. Somehow it worked out for them. Not for Brad and me. If I had had my way, it would have. But I have noticed, when it comes to love, not everyone gets their way.

"Yes, I'll call you," I told Brad, eyeing his gorgeous girlfriend and finding it amusing inside my own head that I was nervous about her seeing him with me, as if someone like her could be jealous of someone like me.

"Tomorrow?"

"Yes, I'll call you tomorrow."

"You won't forget amidst all the calls to the DJ and the caterer and the florist and the photographer, will you?"

"No, I won't forget."

"Are you actually going to be making all those calls?"

"I'm not sure what I will be doing — aside from calling you about this business proposition, of course."

"OK. I'll have to be satisfied with that."

Brad's girlfriend stopped about twenty feet away and was still engrossed in conversation with the attorney couple.

"Care to give me just a little hint?" I said.

"I am working on something that will change the world. In big ways. And you are the perfect person to get in on it."

"And you just happened to realize this when, by some strange quirk of fate, you saw me stuffing my face at the hors d'oeuvre table this evening."

"Yes."

"I see."

"You don't believe stuff like that happens?"

"I don't know. I guess it could."

"What are you working on right now? Professionally, I mean. Not that it matters. Whatever you're working on, you will want to put it aside when you hear my offer."

"Actually, I just finished up my work for a research grant and I have applied for another one. I'm waiting to hear back."

"Wow, you're between jobs. The timing couldn't be more perfect. I'll be waiting for your call, Bel." He smiled, threw his arm in a wide arc, said goodbye, took his girlfriend's arm, shook hands with the attorney couple and guided her toward the door, with his hand pressed lightly on the small of her back.

"I like the other guy better," said the woman in the wheelchair. "He's the real deal."

"But that guy gonna change the world," said the woman with Down syndrome, watching Brad leave. "That cool."

"Who says it's going to be a good change?" said the ruddy woman.

"Yeah, his eyes are hiding something," the woman in the wheelchair noted.

"OK, everyone, that'll do," Marty said. "Let's let this young woman make up her own mind. Maybe the correct answer for her is 'none of the above.'"

"Someone as pretty as her should marry someone handsome like you," said the ruddy woman.

Marty chuckled and blushed shyly, pushing his glasses up on his nose, as he glanced at me. "Well, you got half of that equation right," he told her. "She is pretty."

He knew he was not handsome. You could tell. He carried himself the way someone ordinary would. Despite his solid muscular build, he was, in the face, quite ordinary. Like some folk singer from the late 70's. Collar length hair that wished to curl on the ends, heavy horn-rimmed glasses, that wished to fall down his nose. And yet, something passed through those thick lenses, from his eyes to mine. I wanted to sit with him on a large rock in the woods and listen to him play an Ibanez.

"Do you play guitar?" I heard myself asking him.

And as if this was not at all a strangely random question, he answered, "Yeah, a little bit. Do you?"

"No." I smiled and looked at my shoes. "I can just picture you playing."

"Pretty good intuition," he smiled. "But guitar's not my main instrument. You won't be able to guess what is."

"Sax?"

"No."

"Oboe."

"Nope."

"Clavichord?"

"Don't even know what that one is. Sounds fancy."

"I'm not sure what it is either."

"Give up?"

"Yeah."

"Tuba."

"Hmmm."

"Yeah, that's what all the girls say about tuba players. That's why I took up the guitar. But if you do need a tuba at your upcoming event, I do know how to play the Wedding March."

"I don't know if that will be necessary."

"Well, here," he reached into his pocket and pulled out his wallet. "If you don't care for the tuba, I can play it on the guitar too. Take my card."

"No, I've got nothing against the tuba," I said looking at the card. "It's just that I don't know if I'll be needing the wedding march."

"Oh." He did not seem disappointed.

The card had a large, stylized treble clef, the name "Marty Bender," a phone number and an e-mail address.

"Nice to meet you, Marty." I put my hand out. "I'm Annabel."

His hand was warm and rough. "Annabel Greeley, it's my pleasure."

The pilot announces our gradual descent into Miami. I put my hand in my purse and feel for Marty's card. There's a vertical and horizontal crease where it had once been folded in fours and thrown in the trash. How I wish it had stayed there.

৪৩ ✣ ୯୨

3

Unwind the World

My memory of Aunt Lily is sketchy, but warm. I saw her only a handful of times when I was a kid, but even though our visits were few and brief, I had no doubt she loved me. Only people who love you that much squeeze you that hard.

I remember being afraid of her initially and later annoyed by her and finally ashamed and embarrassed for her. I thought lack of intelligence was a curse, and I found it distressing to be around it. But the year I turned fifteen, I cried when we left after our week-long visit to Aunt Terry's house. Lily and her new husband lived in a guest house in Aunt Terry's backyard and I spent nearly every moment with them. During that particular trip, it began to dawn on me that the word "smart" has multiple definitions.

Although I am what many would consider highly intelligent and "book smart," my mother has always worried about my lack of life skills. Her concern turned out to be a valid one. I don't know if you want to call it a weakness or go so far as to label it a disability. Whatever it is, I suppose it has, to some small extent, on some occasions, affected my quality of life.

I once had a mysterious problem in my computer armoire. Brigades of tiny sugar ants would go marching past my keyboard every night as I typed, along the inside of the cabinet and around behind my monitor. I'd smash them on sight and more would come. Finally, I gave up and opted for peaceful coexistence. Let them march, I decided, as long as they stay clear of my fingers. Then, one day, my computer crashed. I had to take it in to be fixed. While the computer was away, I decided to clean out the armoire. There under the nest of old appointment cards, eyeglasses prescriptions, past-due bills and licked-clean pudding cup lids was the answer to the mystery — the food source that had kept the ants nourished and active for upwards of half a year. Nestled in a gerbil-sized dust bunny was a single Milk Dud. I've heard it said a roach can live indefinitely on a toenail clipping. So who knows how long that morsel of chocolate covered caramel could have sustained the entire colony of ants that had taken over my home office? When I told my mother about this, happy that I had found the source of all the trouble, she was disturbed and dismayed and immediately typed me up a schedule for regularly cleaning things out. I have followed it with some success.

Once a month, before doing bills, I clear off my desk and clean out my armoire. Every three months, I go through my clothes closet, every six months my pantry. My purse is on the schedule for every two weeks, which happened to fall on the day after the grand opening of the facility for the disabled.

I held Marty Bender's card in my hand, trying to decide what excuse I would have to call a tuba player. I could think of none, though I suspected he was probably the nicest person at that event. I had contemplated calling Brad all day, but I decided I would seem desperate if I did. I decided to call nobody and tossed Marty's card in the trash. Brad called late that afternoon.

"Bel, have dinner with me Friday. I want to talk to you about the work I envision for us. It's exciting work, Bel. It's a breakthrough like the world has never seen."

"Well, I'd love to hear all about it, Brad, but unfortunately, I won't be here Friday. I'm going out of town for a wedding."

"Oh, really? Who's getting married? Not you, I hope."

"One of my Aunt Terry's foster kids."

"Well, how long are you staying?"

"Just over the weekend. I'll be back Tuesday."

"I really hate to wait. Let me see. What about Wednesday? I think I can move some things around."

"Wow, you are really hyper about this. I mean, more hyper than usual."

"You have no idea, Bel. When you hear what I have to tell you, you will share my enthusiasm, I am absolutely certain. It's incredible."

"I can't Wednesday."

"Thursday? I have tickets to Phantom, but I've seen it a hundred times."

"I don't want you to miss your show."

"No, it's fine. Frankly, there are a number of things I'd rather be doing than sitting through that thing one more time, including getting a root canal."

"Won't your girlfriend be disappointed?"

"Actually my mother has been wanting to go. I'll just give her my ticket and they can go together."

"OK, It's your life. I'll need to make it an early night though. I'm leaving early the next morning."

"Sure, no problem. I'll pick you up at 6:30, OK?"

"Let's make it 7."

"OK, 7 it is. You still live at the same place?"

"Yup. You remember how to get here?"

"How could I forget the road that leads to you?"

I smiled. It was a reference to "our" song.

The road that leads to you
over mountains, through valleys
around the world a hundred times
If ever it takes me more than a breath away
Unwind the world
make it spin the other way
I will rewind my way back to you

I had suspected that Brad's proposition would include more than a business partnership. He was speaking now in code, and I was half flattered and half annoyed. Now that someone else might marry me, he re-emerges, like a kid who throws his old toys in the corner of the closet for two years and then begs his mom not to give them to the poor when she starts pulling them out and boxing them up.

He will come in and destroy what I have with Logan and then leave. I know that. I know it for sure. He will present me with a career option I can't refuse and that will be the end of Logan. I won't be able to work with one and marry the other. I know Logan is the better man. So, if I were smart, I would tell Brad I am not interested in whatever he has to offer.

"See you Thursday, then," I said.

"Looking forward to it. Very much."

"You want to give me a hint? I'm a bit curious."

"I already gave you a hint. But I'll explain it in detail Thursday. Until then, suffice it to say, I am working on something that will change the course of humanity. I doubt there's ever been any development in all of history that has had so much potential to change society. Change it for the better."

Just as I hung up, Logan called. He had more of a lilt in his voice than usual.

"We have to start thinking about where we want to go on our honeymoon," he said.

"Our honeymoon?"

"Yeah. What's someplace you've never been and always wanted to go?"

"I've always wanted to go to Australia."

"Australia? Why Australia?"

"I don't know. I've wanted to go ever since I was a kid."

"What's there to do there? Besides pet koala bears?"

"Where do you want to go?"

"I was thinking Europe. France is so romantic."

"True."

"Italy has so much character. You and me at a small little villa, sipping wine and sharing a strand of spaghetti."

I know that is supposed to sound fun, but I can't feel

anything at all about it, though I do love Europe.

"But wherever you decide, my love. I will be happy wherever I am as long as I am with you. I know it's traditional for the groom to plan the honeymoon, but I just want you to be happy. So, if you want to go pet koala bears, I'll be right by your side."

Well, it's certainly something you can't do at home. So it passes my father's litmus test on whether it should be done on vacation. When I was a kid, we were never allowed to do anything on vacation that we could do "back home." That means we couldn't, for instance, eat at any chain restaurants. "I didn't pay $2,000 and drive 650 miles so we could eat at Denny's," he'd say. We'd drive and drive to find some one-of-a-kind restaurant, even if it was a dump, even if the dump is right next door to the very nice, very high quality chain, which is a chain for a reason, because it is successful and people like it. No, if it's something we could do back home, we would wait until we were back home. Other kids could play Frisbee on the beach. Not us. Playing Frisbee was something you could do anywhere, including back home. When you were on the beach, you had to do something you could only do on the beach, such as build a sand castle or go surfing. We once got away with playing volleyball though, because you can only play beach volleyball while on the beach. That was my argument and it worked. My siblings considered me brilliant and highly appreciated my intelligence because from that moment on, we were able to use that argument on a number of occasions. We were even allowed to once dine at Spaghetti Factory because we convinced our Dad that, at home, we could not eat spaghetti while looking out the window at Lake Superior.

"Listen, Logan," I say, after our fifteen minutes of discussing which continent is most appealing to romantic couples, "I can't make any decisions right now."

"Of course, of course. We have plenty of time to plan the honeymoon."

"No, I don't mean that, Logan. I mean about marrying

you. I have Tasha's wedding coming up. Let me just get through that first. I'll take some time to think about it."

"What do you have to think about? Don't you love me?"

"Yes, I love you."

"But."

"Yes, but."

"What's the but?"

"I don't know exactly."

"Take me with you to your cousin's wedding."

"I thought you didn't want to go. It's going to be wall-to-wall extended family."

"I can't wait to meet your family."

"You would try to rally them for your cause."

"I wouldn't do that. I know what decision would make me happy, but in the end, I want you to make the one that will make you happy. I just hope those decisions are one in the same."

"I wish they could be, Logan."

"Sounds like you have already made up your mind."

"I don't know."

"Let me come with you anyway. Maybe you'll be able to gather some more information about this poor, hopelessly-in-love fellow who wants nothing more than to make you happy the rest of your life."

I smile.

"Seriously, Anna. You won't find anyone who will love you more than I will. That is my pledge to you. My pledge to your heart. From my heart. I will treat you like a queen for the rest of our lives. I will never let a day go by when I don't get down on my knees, take your hand in mine, kiss it tenderly and ask, 'What can I do to please the love of my life today?'"

"You know I don't require that much maintenance."

"But you deserve it. I've never met a woman like you before, Anna. Pretty, smart, witty. The two of us together, Darling, we would be a force to be reckoned with."

I smile again.

"Have you ever met a better matched couple than we are? Have you met your equal before now?"

I thought about Brad. Then, for some inexplicable reason, I thought of Marty Bender.

"Just hold onto that question, Anna," Logan counseled. "Think about it while you are on your trip. Please, for my sake and yours. Think about it. A woman like you needs her equal. And she won't find it in many places."

৪০�����ৎ

I have to admit, I labored over what to wear for my meeting with Brad. By the time I chose something, I had more clothes on the closet floor than on hangers. No piece of clothing I owned looked quite right with any other piece of clothing I owned. If I were meeting any other guy, I wouldn't have to worry about it. But Brad is different. He notices details and cares what the woman he is with looks like. The first time he took me to meet his family, he asked if he could look through my closet and choose something for me to wear. I later told Logan this, and he found it very strange, maybe even psychologically unsound.

I took the royal blue, long-sleeved, button-down-the-front silk dress off the rack and tried to evaluate it. This is the dress Brad chose for me to meet his family. What was it he liked — or thought his mother would like? I am certain it was all about pleasing her. I haven't worn that dress since. What if I wore it tonight?

I settled on some jeans, high-heeled boots, a white silk blouse, a chain belt and a black cashmere sweater. I didn't want to look like I cared about what I was wearing, so jeans seemed the answer. My mother always says you can't go wrong with jeans, unless you're a bride's maid or the bride. I felt bad that I hadn't even told my mom or dad about Logan's proposal. I wanted to talk to my mom, especially, when the time was right. She could help me sort this all out. She is good at sorting. But, I wasn't ready yet to hear any specific answer, and once your mother weighs in with a particular piece of advice, it is difficult to dismiss it. I wanted to be able to dismiss anything and everything at this point.

I wondered what it must have been like for Logan, growing up without a mother. Logan's mother and brother died in a car accident when he was seven. I have always excused him for his occasional lack of sensitivity because I believe children, for the most part, learn compassion from their compassionate mothers, if they have one. It was just Logan and his father left, and since his father ran a lucrative real estate business and was gone a lot, he paid the neighbor to take care of Logan. The neighbor had three boys of her own and tied her tubes so there wouldn't be a fourth. She took care of Logan for the extra cash, and that was always clear to Logan, at times overtly, at times subconsciously.

As I was blow drying my hair, Brando took off after Daisy and knocked over the trash can. A couple of wadded up tissues and a gum wrapper fell out, along with Marty's card. I was about to re-trash it, but as I held it in my hand, I couldn't bring myself to throw it away. I remembered how happy he was with those disabled people and how happy they were with him. I wondered what he was doing at that moment. Was he feeding someone? Was he playing cards or bingo? Was he tucking someone in bed? What would it feel like to be cared for by him?

ஒஜ்கை

4

Targeting Eggs

I think I must have chosen the right outfit for lunch with Brad. His eyes locked on mine, and his large, boyish grin seemed to refresh something within me. He took me to the Chinese restaurant we always went to on New Year's Eve. We spent four of them together. Beijing Garden was a hole in the wall, comfortable and familiar. Strangely enough, it seemed to me that we had the same waitress.

"It's really great you could meet with me tonight, Bel. You don't know how excited I've been to share this news with someone. Well, not just someone, but you. Specifically."

"Well, I've been in suspense, Brad. What is your news?"

"Let's order first. Will you have a Maotai with me?

"I don't think so, Brad. I've got an early flight tomorrow."

"Oh, just one won't hurt."

The waitress came by, and Brad ordered the drinks and a couple of more minutes to decide on food.

"Are you excited about your trip?" he asked, looking at the menu.

"Yes, it will be nice. Weddings are so much nicer than funerals, and those are pretty much the only reasons we all get together. I am really going primarily to see my cousins, John and Beth. I really miss them."

"Have you decided what you'd like? How about I order our old favorites?"

28

"That would be fine."

"Unfortunately, this food will not be nearly as good as you make."

"Well, I don't do much cooking anymore."

"That's a pity. Does Logan not appreciate great Chinese?"

"He does. But we have so many events lately. Seems like we're never home."

"Do you enjoy all that rubber chicken and dry cheesecake?"

"Not much. That seems like pretty much all you get at those dinners though."

The waitress smiled and bowed to signal she was about to interrupt this talk of inferior banquet food to offer us a better alternative. After she took the order and left us with our Maotais, Brad looked deep into my eyes and held his glass in the air. "To breaking new ground and building a better tomorrow."

I clinked my glass against his and took a sip. "So."

He took a gulp. "OK." And another gulp, then set down his glass. "I am working on a vaccine for women in their child-bearing years. It targets eggs with genetic abnormalities and renders them incapable of being fertilized, resulting in a vast reduction in the number of birth defects."

"Wow."

"I know. It's incredible. It will quite literally change the world."

"Yeah. It would."

"Not would, Bel. *Will*."

"Have you entered the clinical trial phase?"

"Just getting there now. We need to test it over time. Wait for egg to meet sperm a number of times and see what happens. Does it hold out longitudinally? If not, what do we need to modify? That's where you come in, Bel, hopefully. I'm going to need some help. A partner. I figure the timing couldn't be more perfect with your grant expiring. So what do you think?"

"You don't have any reservations about mixing our personal and professional lives?"

"Mixing, no. We're not mixing. This is strictly business."

"And given our past, you don't see that as a bit difficult — to keep it strictly business?"

"No. Not at all. The past is the past. You clearly have moved on. I can too."

"Hmmm. OK."

"Believe me, Bel, I'm interested only in your brain. Not that the rest of you isn't quite appealing too, but I know the score. Honestly, this thing is so all-consuming, I don't have time for a relationship right now. I am completely obsessed with this project. No, *project* is the wrong word. Call it a breakthrough, call it a miracle."

"A vast reduction in Down syndrome, cystic fibrosis —"

"A gamut of congenital conditions. Think of the numbers of people who will be saved from the pain of giving birth to a baby whose life is going to be fraught with difficulties."

"Rid the world of people who would cause somebody emotional or financial hardship." I scratched my head and looked at the couple at the next table. They seemed to be involved in some frivolous conversation, and I was jealous. Something like which store had the best deal this week on boneless, skinless chicken breasts.

"OK, why aren't you excited about this, Bel?"

"I don't know, Brad. I don't know exactly why I'm not excited about it. It just seems to have some ethical questions attached to it."

"Like what? You're not taking anything away from anyone. You're not even destroying life after it's been created. That's what people are doing now. Diagnosing in utero and then taking the life of their unborn, disabled children."

I nodded and took a sip of the clear liquor, wondering why anyone would drink a substance that tastes more like it belongs in a spray bottle than a wine glass. The heat filled my nose and my throat and seeped down my esophagus to my belly.

"So, what do you think?"

"I think I will have to think about it."

"It'll be like old times, Bel. You remember what a great team we made. I've never worked so well with anyone."

"Like old times."

"Bel, I know what you're thinking. You have my word. I will not do anything to mess things up for you and Logan. I know you no longer have feelings for me."

I just stared at him, remembering.

"Or do you? Bel?"

"I don't know, Brad. I don't know if I'm the one you're looking for."

"You are definitely the one, Bel."

"For the project, you mean."

"Is that what *you* meant?"

"You see how complicated this is already? It would never work."

"Why? Bel, do you still have feelings for me?"

"I'm trying to decide that, Brad." I think of Lily and Frank. How simple it all was for them. How happy they were that way. Simple. How they never had to discern. From the moment they met on the plane and discovered their mutual love of roller coasters and the undeniable, unmistakable feeling they were meant for each other. They had a goal to ride a hundred different roller coasters together. They got to eight. True roller coasters, I mean. Not the Space Mountain variety. Some people might say you can't base a relationship on such things, and probably those people are right. But it worked for Lily and Frank.

The year that Millennium Thriller opened, Frank and Lily planned a special trip to California. It was convenient to have Pablo living in California, so they had a place to stay. Frank and Lily wanted to be there on the first day it opened. Frank's work schedule wouldn't allow that, so they ended up going on the second week. Of course, they were not alone. People were willing to wait in ninety-minute lines for the three-minute ride. It was no surprise to Frank and Lily. They had done the research and knew what they were in for. So they brought a sack lunch. Pablo cut their ham sandwiches into fours, knowing they would have to eat while standing. He packed them each a box of animal crackers, a packet of goldfish crackers and a can of V-8. Inside of Lily's sack was a note: "You and Frank have a good time. I love you. Daddy." He printed very clearly, in large letters. Lily never did learn to read cursive. Frank gave Lily all the monkeys he found in his animal cracker box and Lily handed Frank all the tigers. Lily had been a fan of monkeys since she was introduced to Curious George as a little girl. Bananas were the only fruit she would ever eat, and she only ate them because George ate them.

When Lily and Frank had waited in line for an hour and ten minutes, there came an announcement that the coaster was experiencing technical difficulties and would be down indefinitely. Eight coaster riders had become stuck upside down 128 feet in the air and had to be rescued. The coaster had to be tested to a satisfactory level before any more guests would be allowed to ride. Thrill seekers began to discuss whether they should wait or not, with those at the beginning of the line deciding mostly to stay, while those at the end, cut their losses and went to find another ride. Lily and Frank did not need to discuss it. They sat down, arm in arm, Lily resting her head on Frank's shoulder. And that's the way they stayed for the next twenty minutes, until the next announcement came. "Thank you for your patience. We are still experiencing technical difficulties and do not know when the ride will resume." Nothing could have dissuaded Frank and Lily. Ever since it was reported that the Millennium Thriller was under construction the year prior, each one had put fifty cents in an empty cream of wheat box each day, to cover bus fare and admission to the park.

So at each "update" announcement, which provided no information except for that there was no new information, people left the line, and Frank and Lily moved up. After two hours, they were the seventeenth and eighteenth people in line.

They entertained themselves with rounds of rock, paper, scissors.

By now, new people had joined the line and some old line-standers had returned. Everyone was trying to determine a strategy, though all the variables were so variable, strategizing was impossible. Rock, paper, scissors had gotten old, so Frank and Lily switched to one potato, two potato.

After close to three hours, Frank and Lily were rewarded for their patience and their eternally-springing hope and were allowed to board. There was an extra element of thrill as Frank reminded Lily that he himself once got stuck on a roller coaster 120 feet in the air and had to be escorted down by park officials dressed in dark blue coveralls with miniature communication devices pinned to their collars, looking something like they had just stepped off the Starship Enterprise. His ride with Lily, however, went off without a hitch.

The waitress placed our food in the middle of the table and took away the Ming vase-inspired plates before us, replacing them with white stoneware.

Brad asked for chopsticks, and I inquired about how his mother was doing while the waitress went to retrieve some.

"She is fine now. She suffered a minor stroke about six months ago, but it turned out to be nothing serious."

"Oh, that's good. And the rest of your family?"

"Thank you," Brad said to the waitress as she laid the chopsticks at our plates. "The family is great," he said smiling at me. "Yours?"

"Yes, everyone is well, thank God."

For a long moment, Brad stared at me, unused chopsticks in hand.

"What?"

"You are so beautiful, Bel."

"Thank you." I can't say the compliment didn't thrill me a little. Actually, a lot.

"So, Bel, what do you think? About the project."

It has the capacity for so much good, and I have been given the opportunity to be a part of it. A huge part of it. It would make me, at the very least, a footnote in history books. Or I might even have my own paragraph. It would certainly make me rich. It would spare countless people suffering and prevent the breaking of hearts. Isn't this what geneticists go into the field of genetics for?

It would mean less of a drain on society, less stress for families and teachers, less expense for schools, fewer burdens for the government. Why would we want people to be born with difficulties if difficulties can be avoided? So, I am with Brad, when I ask, why am I not ecstatic?

All of this was running through my mind as I wrestled with Peking duck, Moo shoo pork and moo goo gai pan. And finally, the match was over, and the chopsticks had eked out a narrow win over the entrees, and I could move onto my favorite part of the meal — not so much because it is dessert, but because it is eaten with your hands.

I bit into the corner of the cookie and felt a small sharp pain in my tooth. I wondered what they made fortune cookies out of. Why are they so hard? Is the paper baked right in or inserted after? How do they make them all look exactly the same? Why is it that no other cookie in the entire world tastes like a fortune cookie? I decided that, when I had a spare moment, I would look up "how fortune cookies work."

"Um. What does it mean when you open one of these and find nothing in it?" I asked Brad, showing him the empty shell.

"Oooh. Creepy. It means all those end-of-the-world prophecies just might be correct."

"It means something's missing from the future." I crunched the cookie between my molars and felt another sharp pain. "And we'll never know what it is."

₧✲₨

5

At the Bottom of the Hill

I dread the tarmac. I am usually anxious for the landing gear to hit the runway, but I don't want to move from my seat. I know there's no other way to catch the connecting flight home to Boston, but that's not where I want to go. I want to keep flying.

I'll have close to two hours at Miami International. Maybe I'll visit the gift shop and try to find a snow globe. I guess it would actually be a sand globe in Florida. My little cousin Miranda has an impressive collection. My favorite is the one I got her in London — snow falling on Big Ben with an iconic red double-decker bus, horribly out of scale, sitting out in front. The latest in her collection was the Space Needle. I bought it for her at the airport before I left Seattle after Tasha's wedding. She was holding it up and shaking it at me with one hand and waving madly at me with the other as I walked down the jet way to board the plane. I got a call a few minutes after we had reached cruising altitude. It was Beth telling me that Miranda insisted on talking to me. When Beth passed her the phone, Miranda was crying so hard I could scarcely tell what she was trying to say. Something about wrestling the Space Needle out of Lucy's hand and somebody fumbling, sending it crashing to the ground and being too far away from the airport now to turn around and go get another one. She explained how distraught she was because it was one of her most favorite out of all her extensive collection, which includes the Eiffel tower, the San Francisco Bridge, the Liberty Bell, the Vatican, the Alamo, the White House, the Washington Monument, Mount Rushmore,

Santa on the beach playing volleyball with his reindeer, and Belle and Aurora having tea together.

Belle has always been my favorite Disney princess, not because she shares my name and likes to read, but because she puts aside her own well-being to save the two men she loves — first her father and then the beast.

I watched *Beauty and the Beast* practically every day of my life from the age of three until I turned five. Why, then, was self sacrifice not engrained in me, not part of my instincts when my moment came?

How long did it take me to make the calculation that my life was worth more than his? How did I come to the conclusion so quickly — that I should let him die to keep myself out of harm's way? Somewhere in my inner being the decision was made, in a split second, in less time than it takes to blink, I made the decision to do nothing.

Lily was hit by a bus when she was in her 30s. I wonder if anyone thought of pushing her out of the way. Did they, too, make a split-second calculation that her life was worth less than theirs? That she would contribute less to humanity, accomplish less for the betterment of society?

The passengers file past as the man on the aisle gathers his bags from the overhead compartment. One couple, young and beautiful, pass arm in arm. I imagine they are newlyweds, returning from a Jamaican honeymoon. They have that same look that Tasha and Oscar had as they left the reception hall — sort of child-like, with dewy faces, eyebrows raised in optimistic arcs, like two people who had just awoken from the same dream, only to realize their waking life is even more sublime. It's hard to believe it's been a month since Tasha's wedding.

I was originally not planning to attend since none of my immediate family would be there. But the Lovely family, and everything that sprang forth from it, seemed to have the greatest concentration of love I had ever seen anywhere, and I needed some of it. I also needed to understand it. I decided I would make it a point to grill every happily married person I knew about this question of love. My cousins Beth and her father, Jake, were first, since I happened to be sitting with them on Beth's back porch the Friday afternoon before the wedding rehearsal, eating from an assortment of cheese and vegetable and fruit trays prepared by Costco.

"The key is knowing what's really important in life," Uncle Jake offered. "Don't sweat the small stuff. If she wants Berber carpet and you want pile, you go with the Berber and get yourself some nice memory foam slippers."

"Spoken like the husband of an interior designer," I said.

"Well, your Aunt Terry can have some pretty strong ideas about what she wants."

"That's for sure," said Beth, biting into a piece of pineapple on a toothpick.

"But I have learned to appreciate that, since she's the one with the vision," Uncle Jake continued. "She's the one who gets stuff done. Like, right now, for instance, she's the one over there making preparations at the church, and I can guarantee you, it will be pretty, and Tasha will feel like she's died and gone to heaven when she first lays eyes on it." He took a swig of vitamin water and wiped his mouth with the back of his hand. Uncle Jake is probably the most handsome man I've ever seen in his age group. Actually, in all age groups. That's from an objective observer's point of view. I know there are many women who would find him too perfect, with a face that lacks flaws and therefore lacks character. That's how Brad is, to a lesser degree. Logan, however, has a face you want to study because you haven't seen anything like it. A painter would find joy in painting it, with its sharp and unpredictable lines. I have to admit, I find joy in looking at it, and I would miss it a great deal if I never got a chance to see it again.

"But I'm not just talking crepe paper," Uncle Jake clarified. "I'm talking about the important stuff. We wouldn't have Tasha and we wouldn't have John if it wasn't for Terry having a vision and seeing it through. At all costs. You might think someone like that would be hard to live with. And you know what? You'd be right. But I wouldn't trade anything that's happened to me since I met that woman."

"Sweet," I smiled. "How about you, Beth? How did you know Michael was the one?"

"Well, probably mostly because when I was with him, I wasn't on the outside looking in on myself, critiquing how I delivered my lines. Life just unfolded, and I unfolded with it. Up to that point, I was watching myself walk through this world. I was listening to the words that came out of my mouth. I was making evaluations and drawing conclusions based on what I saw and heard. But when I was with Michael, there was just Michael and my complete absorption into the space around him. I guess that's what people call the ability to be yourself. I would call it the ability to forget yourself. And that was a real relief because my self was a real handful and very exhausting and time consuming."

"How did you meet?"

"We met at seminary?"

"Seminary?"

"We were both visiting seminarians. Michael was visiting his brother and I was visiting the man I wanted to marry."

"You wanted to marry a man who was studying to be a priest?"

"Desperately."

"And what became of him?"

"He became Father Daniel DiCiccio, who will be concelebrating at the wedding tomorrow."

"Your ex-boyfriend is marrying Tasha and Oscar?"

"I don't know if boyfriend is accurate." She looked closely at a grape on her toothpick and then popped it in her mouth. "Savior maybe?"

"Savior."

"Yes," she nodded. "Savior. That would be accurate."

I could use one of those right now as I trudge though Miami International to catch a connecting flight between a past I wish I could erase and a future I have no idea how to live. I don't think I would ever call Logan anyone's savior. I know for absolute certain Brad is not. Marty showed his willingness to lay down his life for someone right before my eyes. Isn't that what a savior does? But he and I were apparently not meant to be. For a while there, I wondered if we might be.

Standing at the gate, waiting for someone to disembark, is a long-haired, grey-bearded man in a Harley Davidson T-shirt. Reminded me of Dad's stories of Two Dog Dan.

Every Christmas, Two Dog Dan came by to bring Frank and Lily a box of Whitman's Samplers. He'd park his Harley at the sidewalk and tromp to the front door, chains rattling, black leather squeaking past the Azaleas. He'd knock *shave and a haircut two cents* and then shift from foot to foot and steady himself, as if Hulk Hogan might be on the other side of that door. Frank would fling the door open and the two would embrace like a couple of grizzlies, and Lily would come running and join in the clasp.

It took several years for Frank to remember to include Two Dog on his Christmas list, so Two Dog would receive an impromptu gift of a Class A specimen from Frank's stick collection. On subsequent years, Frank and Lily gave him Hot Wheels motorcycles.

You might ask, how does a guy like Two Dog Dan become friends with people like Frank and Lily? In the usual way. They met at a pool hall.

Frank and Lily got a miniature pool table with pearlescent pool balls as a wedding gift. They'd play every night. They had their own set of rules that varied a bit from the standard. First off, if you didn't get a ball in, you could keep trying until you did. Then it was the next person's turn. Second, Frank was not allowed to hit the pink ball or the 3 ball in because those were Lily's favorite color and number. Lily was not allowed to sink the silver or the 7. Their rules had to be adjusted the day a pool hall opened up next to the bowling alley where Frank worked. There were no pink or silver balls there.

The very first time Frank and Lily walked into the Lucky Q, there were whispers and sideways glances. Behind the counter, there was a young petite and muscular fellow wearing a muscle shirt and tight blue jeans and a gold ID bracelet. He reluctantly reached out his hand when Frank handed him a $20 bill. He leaned forward and spoke in a low voice. "Just to let you know, buddy. This is kind of a rough place sometimes. I don't know if this is where you're gonna wanna hang out."

"Don't worry. We love pool."

"And we very good," Lily added.

Witnessing the conversation was a man with a pit bull wearing an army helmet tattooed on his left arm and a bulldog wearing rabbit ears tattooed on his right. The man vowed to make sure no one messed with these two particular newcomers. This man had a lot of friends, all of whom rode Harleys and many of whom played pool regularly, thus rendering the Lucky Q as safe as the Lovely living room. For Frank and Lily at least. The rest of the customers took their chances.

Two Dog Dan would later reveal to Lily's family, as he sat with them at Christmas Eve dinner, that his kid brother had Down syndrome and passed away 23 years ago when they were teenagers. Frank reminded him of what his kid brother might have grown up to be.

"Man, I miss that kid." He rested his fork in his mashed potatoes and stared into his plate.

Everyone else stopped eating too, glancing around at each other. They were all afraid Two Dog Dan was going to cry. And they were all asking themselves what they would do if he did. Then Lily got up from the table and wrapped her arms around his neck from the back and Frank came to the other side and put his arm around him. Two Dog sniffed and nodded largely, rubbed his eyes with his forefinger and thumb and picked up some potatoes with his fork. "I'm OK. I'm OK."

"What was his favorite Christmas song?" asked Terry

Lovely.

"*Jingle Bell Rock*."

"What yours?" Lily asked Two Dog.

"*Jingle Bell Rock*." Two Dog smiled, flashing his gold tooth, making the leather around his moist eyes fold into stiff accordions.

"Mine is *Let it Snow*," Lily offered.

"Me too!" Frank exclaimed, as if he had just discovered this, when in fact, he and Lily pressed repeat on that song and played it nonstop in their home from Advent until Epiphany.

After Jake had left to get ready for the wedding rehearsal, I stayed to help Beth clean up and get her little ones ready. Michael was over at the hall, setting up tables for the reception.

"Beth, I'd like to get your opinion on something else," I said combing the blonde soft curls at the nape of Lucy's neck.

"Sure. I have opinions on all things. Pretty much."

"What would you think of a vaccine to prevent conception in eggs carrying the genetic code for birth defects."

"You mean like Down syndrome?"

"Aunt Lily had Down syndrome," said Lucy, sounding quite knowledgeable.

"Among many others," I said.

"Have you ever read Beverly Greeley's letter to your mother?"

"Yes. A number of times."

"You know then?"

"Know what? About Lily? Oh, yes, I know all about Lily. You can't be born into this family without knowing all about Lily, as little Lucy here has clearly demonstrated." I crane my head around the front of her and give her a smile. "We hear about her constantly. My dad tells the same stories about her over and over again."

"Did he ever tell you that you owe your life to her?"

"I surmised that from Bev's letter."

"I will tell you Lily would not have been better off not

existing. And none of us would have been better off without Lily. As a matter of fact, you and I have something in common. If it wasn't for Lily, I might not be alive either."

"Really?"

"Yeah. It's a long story. But if it hadn't been for Lily, I might have taken my own—" She cocked her head toward Lucy, signaling that she couldn't say any more.

"Oh, yeah," I said. "I remember you talking about that at her funeral."

"Not only that, but if it wasn't for Lily, I never would have met Michael, and I wouldn't have my three amazing and exasperating children. I only met Michael because I met Danny. And I only met Danny because of Lily."

"Why? Was she dating him too?" I smiled.

"He was her shrink."

"What's a shrink?" Lucy wrinkled her nose. "Is that someone who shrinks you, so you can go down the rabbit hole like Alice in Wonderland?"

"Actually," Beth continued, "I wouldn't have met Michael if it wasn't for Father Fitz, who somehow inspired Danny to explore his vocation at a dedication of an animal shelter opened in Lily's honor after her death. By the way, you are going to get to meet Father Fitz. He and Father Danny are going to be concelebrating the wedding"

"Oh, I remember Father Fitz. Didn't he marry Lily?"

"Father Fitz? I love Father Fitz! He gives us gum!"

"Oooh, what kind?" I asked, tying a pink ribbon in one of the ponytails I had made.

"Juicy Fruit and sometimes Big Red."

"Do you remember Lily's wedding, Annabel?" Beth asked. "You were pretty young."

"I remember the church full of lilies. And I remember how pretty Lily looked." I went to work on Lucy's other hair bow.

"It was a beautiful wedding. And very Lily."

"What do you mean?"

"Like when Pablo kissed her hand just before he gave her away, and then she kissed both of his hands."

"How sweet. That's the way I remember Lily."

"Oh, and on the wedding video, you can see Pablo walking her down the aisle to give her away and she's smiling and waving at everyone, like she is some kind of royalty greeting her loyal subjects. Then, she gets up to the front, and Frank's mother drops her tissue near the aisle, and Lily stops the procession and the waving, bends down, picks it up and gives it back to her. And that moment became kind of a symbol of their relationship. Lily tried very hard to please that woman, who had, all her life, assumed that she was being punished with a child like Frank."

"Really? How sad for Frank."

"Mommy, can I go play now?" Lucy asked.

"Sure, but don't mess up your hair. Cousin Annabel did such a pretty job."

"OK. I won't."

"Tell your sister to come get her hair done."

"Which one?"

"All of her hairs."

"No, I mean which sister?"

"Miranda. Leslie is old enough to do her own hair."

"Even for a wedding rehearsal?"

"Sure."

"Then, how come Tasha is getting her friend to do hers?"

"Because Tasha's friend is a professional."

"Oh. OK." She ran from the kitchen and was immediately called back in.

"Is there something you'd like to say to Annabel?"

"Thank you for doing my hair." She said it with a slight curtsy that made her seem like a kid from a 1940s movie.

"You're welcome. It was my pleasure." I curtsied too.

"Anyway," Beth said, turning the water back on to continue scrubbing the coffee pot, "Frank's mother had always wanted kids and could never get pregnant until, one day, when

43

she was in her mid-forties. And along came Frank."

"And she was disappointed," I said, pulling hair out of the brush and wrapping it around my finger.

"For the rest of her life. Well, no, not for the rest of her life. For the rest of *his* life. Things actually improved between them after he died."

I didn't get a chance to ask how exactly that was possible.

"Oh, my goodness, Annabel," Beth said, drying the lid to the coffee pot. "I've got to go pick up the cake. You're welcome to come. Or make yourself at home here."

"Thanks, but I think I will go for a long walk. It's such a pretty day. And then come back and take a long bath. Unless you need me to do something."

"No, I'm quite certain we've got everything covered, right down to the number of bird seeds each guest will receive to throw at the bride and groom. You would be fortunate to have the Lovely machine kick in and plan your wedding when it's your turn. This thing will go off without so much as a hiccup, thanks to my mother."

It was, however, discovered less than fifteen minutes later, that someone had misplaced the bag of 150 plastic Champaign flutes for the best man toast, and it would be quicker to go buy more than to search everyone's trunk and garage for the ones that had already been purchased. That's how I ended up walking through the aisles of Costco, wondering what love is. I know it seems like a basic question. I have been able to comprehend and grasp all these intricate and complex workings of the human body, down to the smallest unit of what comprises humanity, but I am baffled by the basics. That, to me, makes life very strange, almost unmanageable.

Of course, you can't go to Costco and just buy what you came for. At least I've never known anyone who could. So I decided to peruse the assortment of cereals in hopes of finding several varieties that Beth's kids might like. I could maybe establish myself as the cousin who brings sugary cereal and therefore the cousin whose arrival is joyfully awaited.

'You're full of crap," declared a coarse voice behind me coming around the corner into my aisle. "Most of the time."

I turned to see a wide old lady toddling behind her cart, with a skinny old man smiling by her side. "I am," he agreed, proudly. They both had the same smirks on their faces. "Give me some Bisquick," she said pointing in front of her.

"Huh?"

"Bisquick," she bellowed.

"Oh, Bisquick!"

"What did you think I said, you deaf old man?"

"I thought you said give me a biscuit. I was looking around for a biscuit." They were both smiling at the ridiculousness of that misunderstanding. "I thought maybe they were sampling biscuits somewhere."

"Ughhhhhh. You are a piece of work."

I wondered if they had played with each other like this all their lives. How did they hold onto it so long? How did it not become stale? For a second, it crossed my mind that they might be siblings instead of spouses. I quickly ruled that theory out. Something told me they had once had some magnetism between them. A forty-year-old picture of them came to me — a young couple sharing passionate kisses on a moonlit bridge. But there they were decades later, with all that gone, facing the end of their lives, with the reality of many annoyances and irritable moments, as her health declines and she struggles to walk and he has to wait on her, fulfill her every need, because she can't even lift her hands off the cart and pick a box of Bisquick off the shelf. And his failing hearing that makes her repeat everything three times so she doesn't end up with a biscuit instead of Bisquick. They had that easy way of being together that was completely devoid of pretense or civility. They knew each other too well to mess with pleasantries. The romance was obviously long gone — all the dopamine that's released in your brain when you're falling in love — all evaporated years ago. How beautiful, I thought. I want that. Not yet. But someday. Right now, I want dopamine. But someday, I want what that old couple has. You always see those pretty pictures of those old couples walking hand in hand on the beach or down a leafy road together. And that's supposed to be the symbol of enduring love. But that never rang true to me. That feisty, gritty old lady and wise-cracking husband of hers, verbally sparring in a warehouse supermarket — that, to me, is the icon of true love.

ဆာၵာၵာၵာၵာၵာၵာ

Upon delivering the Champaign flutes to the reception hall, I found Beth there, stocking the fridge with drinks. "What do you think Lily felt for Frank?" I asked, using her car keys to slice into the cartons of soda she had yet to open.

"I don't know. Something deep and something simple, I would guess."

"I just don't understand how you know the stuff you're feeling for someone is the stuff you're supposed to be feeling. How do you know that what you have at any given moment is not just a dim shadow of the real thing?"

"Some people say if you have to ask that, it's not the real thing."

"Is that what Lily would say?"

"No. Nothing that complicated. She would probably tell you to marry the one who makes you feel happy when you're with him. And happy when you think about him. Lily would have said 'keep it simple' but love never seems simple. At least it never has been to me. I once thought I'd found the man I wanted to spend the rest of my life with and he ended up leading me to the man I would spend the rest of my life with."

"And you are happy?"

"Yes. Exceedingly. Michael makes me smile."

"And then I keep asking myself, why even get married? What does it all mean? What will it mean?"

"It means a good deal of suffering. A fair amount of heartache. And healthy portions of irritation and aggravation. I mean, think about it. The person you're with is the best he'll ever be right now. He's not going to get any more handsome or any smarter or any more charming as the years go on. And you're not going to either. You and him, you're on a downhill slope. But at the bottom of the hill, you're going to be there for each other. That takes a fair amount of sacrifice and wisdom and understanding and generosity."

"What if you regret the choice you made? You're just stuck."

"I love Michael with all my heart, but I will be honest and tell you, there have been days I regretted the decision to get married. Things would have been a lot simpler flying solo. Not many days of regret, mind you, but there have been days, and I assume we're no different from any other married couple, and if they were going to honest, they'd tell you the same thing."

"So, you still haven't answered my question. Why do it?"

"Because love isn't about what you can get. It's about what you give. It's about sacrifice."

"And why is that something people sign up for?"

She had that look like I had finally asked her a question that, not only had no answer, but had never been asked before. But I forgot for a moment that Beth is Terry Lovely's daughter, so she was able to reach inside to some deep place and materialized this: "To be part of something bigger. Something immeasurable by time and space. Only in giving yourself away can you become fully what you were created to be. Only in losing yourself to that great expanse, in casting yourself into that vast ocean of love and heartache and pain and joy can you hope to emerge as the true you."

"I knew you were an artist, Beth, but I never knew you were a poet. Makes me want to call Logan right now and tell him 'yes.'" A million times yes, my love.

෨✴ର

47

6

Sticks

After delivering the Champaign flutes, there was still
time for a hike. As I walked the trail, through the trees, I
imagined Frank and Lily walking ahead of me. They were arm-
in-arm, smiling at each other as they talked and occasionally
stopped to give each other a kiss on the cheek. Michael
recommended this trail, which was often traversed by Frank and
Lily. In fact, he said, it was the place where Frank got most of
his sticks for his collection.

"I am following a couple of pros," I thought. "These two
people have mastered the art of love. Or is it a craft?" Art
involves creating something new, something that has never been
before. A craft is learned from someone else and can be
mastered, but no crafter can take the credit for his creation
because he himself did not conceive it. It was conceived in the
mind of someone who came before him.

I thought about how Frank and Lily might stop on this
trail to shower each other with bright yellow and orange leaves
in the fall and throw snowballs at each other in the winter and
how Frank might stop and pick wildflowers for Lily's hair in the
spring. I was at a loss for what summer might have meant for
them on this trail, but I know love is for all seasons, so it must
have brought something unlike the rest of the year.

I tried to imagine following behind Frank and Lily with
my hand in Logan's. I don't know that I felt any particular
emotion about that, except maybe unruffled quietude, if that is,

indeed, an emotion. And then I thought of walking with Brad through the seasons. My stomach registered a twinge of elation, followed by a feeling I've only gotten once and that was during a panic attack while driving down switchbacks and hairpins from Flagstaff to Sedona, Arizona, with seven more miles descending ahead of me and the sudden recollection that the last time I took the car in, they had recommended new brakes. It is supposed to be one of the most beautiful drives in the country, and I couldn't enjoy one second of it. I surmised that my stomach was telling me life with Brad would be that kind of ride.

ಬ೫ಅ೫ಬ೫ಅ೫ಬ೫ಅ೫ಬ೫ಅ

I went to the wedding rehearsal that evening just to be with family, most especially John, whom Oscar chose as his best man. John is one of the sweetest people I've ever known. He not only smiles constantly, but he laughs at pretty much anything you say and anything he says. No one would ever guess he struggles with depression. I only know because he confided in me once. He said he is unsure he will ever get married because he doesn't want to bring anyone else into his occasional but very dark misery. I told him he'll reconsider when he meets the right woman, the one who understands that some things are worth suffering for.

I think back on the wisdom of that comment, and I wonder why I have never been able to apply it to my own life. I am not brave enough to choose to suffer, and I don't think I ever have been. There was a split second in time when I specifically chose not, and that choice did irreparable harm. I don't think I will ever get past the grief of that. I don't even know if a hug from John could bring me any comfort, like it did that day, before Tasha's wedding, only a few weeks ago, when I was running away from far easier things.

John and I sat in the garden outside the Church together as the wedding coordinator worked with the Bride's maids.

"I'm glad you came, Annabel," John said. "I didn't think you were going to."

"Well, I'm actually looking for something."

"What?"

"Answers. To some difficult questions."

"What are they? I've pretty much always been your answer man. So, fire away."

"OK. But I warn you. This first one's a tough one."

"Try me."

"What is true love?"

"True love. True love. Well, let me see now." He rubbed his chin and looked at something invisible above and to the right of his head. "OK, I've got it." He nodded and told me this story:

When Frank got sick, Lily was sad that he couldn't get to church. Frank wasn't sad, mind you. But Lily was.

Despite all the offers from family to help him get dressed and get into the car, Frank did not want to go anywhere, including Mass. He had added the supposedly worn-out kneelers to his long list of tirades that he embarked on at least twice daily. He claimed nails came up through them and poked him in the knees.

He was not always so hostile to the Faith. In fact, he was quite committed before his dementia. No one knew how he got the ideas for the little pious rituals he made up. For instance, after Mass, he would stand straight and tall and lift the Bible over his head and bow to the altar. It seemed like something everyone had done for thousands of years. It seemed like something everyone should do.

But the dementia seemed to have robbed him of something, not only in his relationships with other human beings, but also in his relationship with his maker. One day, after Communion, Lily was sitting there without Frank, who was home in bed, and John saw a light bulb go on over her head when the priest made the announcement that those bringing Communion to the sick should come forward.

She sat on the edge of her seat and propped her hand on the pew in front of her, as if she was readying herself for a quick getaway. She watched as two women in their 60s and an elderly man who walked with a cane accepted into their hands pyxes containing the body of Christ and zipped the shiny gold vessels into pouches hanging around their necks. Lily rose from her seat, and proceeded down the aisle toward the altar as if some invisible and irresistible force was pulling her to itself. John sat with his mouth open, not knowing what to do, like someone watching a mid-air collision, helpless to alter the course of events that would ensure disaster. Lily held out her hand to the priest, who leaned in close to her ear and whispered something that made Lily nod and smile. She returned to her seat with a bouncy gait and plopped onto the pew with an unfading smile.

After Mass, Lily led John to the Sacristy, where the priest signed the two up to be trained in bringing Communion to the sick. When John had to go back to school in the fall, Beth and Terry took turns as Lily's assistant.

Lily would hold her hands up to the priest, cupped together as if she were receiving some treasured flow of sacred water. The priest would place the pyx in her hands and she would close her eyes and slowly elevate it to her lips. In those moments, it was not as if Lily was kissing something, John attested. It was as if she was kissing someone. She would place the pyx into its pouch and stick it under her shirt and hold her hands over it the entire way home.

"How come people don' bow down when I carry Jesus?" she often wanted to know. "They jus' walk by Him."

The first time she brought Frank communion, she tripped on the front porch stoop and nearly fell flat in her haste.

"Look, Frank, look what I brought you, Frank. It's Jesus. I brought Jesus to you."

"Where is He? Let me see Him."

"OK, Frank. Here. Here He is." She unzipped the pouch and showed him the pyx.

Frank looked confused for a moment. Then a look of recognition overtook his face. A smile broke out as if he had finally remembered an old friend.

"The body of Christ!" he said.

"No, Frank," Lily corrected. "That what *I* suppose to say.

You suppose to say 'amen.'"

"I know. Amen."

"No Frank, you gotta wait til I say 'Body of Christ.'"

"Well, say it."

"John has to read to you first. From the Bible."

"Why can't I just have Jesus?"

"Hush, Frank. Listen to the Bible. Go ahead, John."

The Gospel that day was about the house built on a rock and the house built on sand.

Lily placed the host on Frank's tongue and kissed his forehead.

And that's what Lily did each of the next fifteen to twenty times she brought Frank Communion.

One day, after the kiss, Frank took her by the hand.

"Lily, I'm going to see Jesus soon. I mean, the Jesus with legs and arms. Not Jesus in the bread. I will say hello from you."

"OK. Where are you going to see Him?"

"In heaven, silly woman."

"Tomorrow?"

"I don't know. Maybe Tuesday. Maybe Wednesday. Maybe Saturday."

"No, Frank. Not soon. I don't want you to go soon."

Frank went to see Jesus that Friday.

John pulled up his pant legs and stretched his socks up to the midway point on his calves. "That is love, Annabel. That is love."

I wondered which part of that story he was referring to. I decided I would think about it some more later and then ask him some time if I couldn't figure it out on my own.

"And how are you doing, John?" I picked up his hand. "I've missed you so much."

"Life is good."

"Are you good?"

"Yeah. Some days not as good as others. But it's a beautiful world, and I'm glad I'm in it."

"Are you still struggling?"

"Not as much right now."

"That's good."

"Yeah, but even when I am, life is beautiful. Even on the days when I can't see the beauty, life is beautiful."

I looked deep into his eyes, hoping to dive into some kind of understanding of what he was saying.

"Being around children teaches you that," he said. "I've been spending a lot of time lately with Beth's kids, and I have learned there's no better way to spend your time."

"Yeah, I know what you mean. I wish I had kids."

"You will someday."

"I hope so."

"I heard you were getting married," he said.

"You did? Where did you hear that?"

"Is it a secret? Tasha told us."

"How did she hear that?"

"I don't know. Is it not true?"

"I don't know. Brad wants me to work with him. Logan wants me to marry him. I can't do both."

"Why not?"

"You know my history with Brad."

"And you still have feelings for him."

"Feelings. Yes. Love, hate, indigestion."

"And what about Logan."

"Just love for Logan."

"Shouldn't that win out?"

"I guess."

"You're not going to pass up the love of your life for a job opportunity, are you?"

"No. I wouldn't do that. I'm just not sure I want to marry Logan in the first place."

"And if you don't marry Logan you are free to pursue the career Brad has to offer."

"I'm not sure I would do that either." I gave him the nutshell version. He wrinkled his forehead and looked at the Church door as he spoke to me. "You know, one day they might come up with a way of identifying that an egg has the genetic coding for depression. And then only happy people will be born."

"And you wouldn't be here."

"Right. And neither would Buzz Aldrin, Hans Christian Andersen, Winston Churchill, John Denver and Fyodor Dostoyevsky. And Abraham Lincoln. And Isaac Newton. I always think to myself, if I'm in the company of all these great artists and scientists and statesmen, why the heck don't I have anything astounding and brilliant to show for it?"

"You are brilliant, John. Why do you think I'm asking you all these tough questions?"

"To which there seems to be some very tough answers. Humans are all about alleviating and eliminating human suffering. Some days, I would tell you there's absolutely nothing wrong with that. But at what cost? It sounds kind of crazy, but there's always a cost to eliminating a cost."

"So there is a cost to alleviating suffering before it even begins?"

"Suffering is the thread from which the stuff of joy is woven. Never will the optimist know joy."

"See? You are brilliant."

"Oh, that's not my quote. That's from Henri de Lubac. He was a French Jesuit. Those guys are brilliant."

"The French or the Jesuits."

"Both."

"But why can't an optimist know joy?"

"Because an optimist assumes everything is going to go right. And we all know that's not how it works."

"Do you ever wish you had never been born?"

"Sometimes. But then the sun comes up the next morning."

"And if, one day, the sun doesn't come up?"

"Then I will be a full participant in the human experience. I have seen the sun and I have seen the darkness. But I will remember the sun. I say this, mind you, on a sunny day, so it's much easier to say. I probably won't tell you the same thing in the dark."

I probably looked confused. He hugged me into him with one arm. "Do you wish I had never been born?" he asked.

"Of course not. You are, so many times, the bright spot in my day. Just thinking about you makes me smile. Makes me know everything is going to be alright."

"Then, maybe that's the reason I was born, old defective genes and all."

"Your genes are perfect as far as I'm concerned. And I'm a professional, so I should know."

"What about Lily's? Were hers perfect?"

I looked off into the garden.

"Or Frank's?"

I focused in on one particular rose, a coral color, so fresh it looked like velvet. John looked with me.

"I used to have a blast with Frank," he said with a broad smile. "He was such a cool guy. We used to play pool together all the time. Sometimes, he beat me."

John arose and walked to the garden, stepped over the low wrought iron gate and into the mulch. He picked up a stick, twisted and gnarled as if it had come from an ancient olive tree from the Holy Land.

"Wow," I said. "I wish Frank were here to see that one."

It wasn't just that Frank loved sticks. It had moved far beyond that. Frank was a professional. Whenever he met someone new, he would introduce himself by saying, "Hi I'm Frank. I collect sticks."

Lily had never known anyone who collected sticks. She had never given sticks much thought. But after she met Frank, she understood why someone would devote his life to it.

Frank kept his stick collection in no less than seventeen spots around the house, including under the bed, on two shelves of the medicine cabinet and inside three kitchen drawers. But his finest specimens were displayed in a Seattle Mariners trash can in the middle of the coffee table. A striking centerpiece it did make, with its fabulous array of long and short, stubby and slender, straight and gnarled, debarked and undefiled. Many were harvested from neighbors' yards, gleaned on the way to work at Sunset Lanes bowling alley. Or on the way back. A few were from city parks and national forests (he had to smuggle those, so they took on a particular appeal). Most were from the local hiking trail. Frank tried to obtain at least one stick from every new place he'd go on vacation. The one in the middle of the trash can arrangement was the tallest. And the most prized. Lily had given it to him on their wedding night. It wasn't a groom's gift really. Groom's gifts require a certain amount of planning and Lily had not planned this one. But it was, she believed, and he believed, inspired. It was procured shortly after they stole out into the breezy moonlit courtyard to escape the crowd of wedding guests and share a quiet, music-less slow dance. When Frank dipped Lily, she gazed up into the trees, and that's when she noticed that the leaves frolicking before the face of the moon were shaped like hearts. Lily took this as a sign that she was to give Frank a branch from that romantic redbud tree.

"Lif- me up, Frank," she demanded.

"Why?" he asked. "I don't have to carry you until we get to the hotel room."

"No, silly. Lif- me in the tree."

"The tree?"

"Jus- lif- me up, Frank."

Now, normally Frank had no difficulty picking Lily up. It had to be the slipperiness of the silk against the excessiveness of the taffeta that led to the tumble, interpreted by hotel management as a couple who was uninformed that it is customary to wait until you get behind closed doors to begin the honeymoon.

In any case, it was doubtful that anyone outside the wedding party accepted the very logical and innocent explanation for why the bride was found straddling the flattened groom, both laughing hysterically, she stroking his hair. Believable or not, the story so endeared the couple to the hotel management that maintenance was directed to bring a ladder and a saw. Frank had the pick of any branch he wanted (within reach of a very short groundskeeper standing on a very tall ladder.) He let Lily choose. She insisted he pick. He refused. She chose the one with the most offspring branches.

Although Lily never had an appreciation for sticks before she met Frank, she did understand the joy of collecting stuff. Lily had a tooth collection. It started with John's baby teeth and grew over the years to include those of great nieces and nephews. After she met Frank, she started adding the teeth of other species to her collection, starting with shark's teeth from Seattle Aquarium, where Frank took her on their first wedding anniversary as a tribute to their goldfish, Bubbles, who had died the day before and was buried in a shallow grave in the back yard. Frank took two of his most prized sticks and, using 18 inches of twine, made a cross and pushed it into the ground in the flower bed outside their guest house. Lily asked Father Fitz to come for a graveside service, but he was busy saying a funeral Mass for a human. Lily understood.

Father Fitz had been a good friend to Lily. He married her and Frank and then went to court to fight against the couple's sterilization, which had become mandatory for people with "diminished mental capacities." Father Fitz testified that the practice impedes the couple's right to exercise their conscience and violates their religious freedom. Since they could not afford an attorney, Father Fitz acted as their legal counsel. He had no prior courtroom experience, but he had watched more than his share of courtroom dramas and documentaries. He won the case.

Though their love was fruitful in many ways, no children ever came to Frank and Lily.

For the most part, Frank and Lily's days went by in the same uneventful fashion that most all people's days do. Then there was the occasional reminder that Frank and Lily were not "most people." Like the day the gate agent refused to let them board the plane. It was Frank's fault, at least according to Lily's retelling. Frank was laughing too loud. Frank insisted it was Lily's fault. For making him laugh. It was the latest in a long string of knock-knock jokes that pushed him over the edge into a realm of hysteria from which he could not recover, no matter how hard he tried. It didn't help that Lily was giggling as well, and no sooner had he composed himself than he would glance her way again, and they would both erupt in hysterics.

At any rate, it was all too much for the grim boarding agent who alternated between two questions: Number one, was it in their power to settle themselves down and put whatever it was that was so funny out of their minds until the final leg of their trip was finished? And number two, did either of them have an attendant? The answer to both of these questions was no. At the point when they could compose themselves, they would be able to board, she told them. But as Lily stood with her back to the terminal window, flight 412 lifting into the sky behind her, she and Frank were still embroiled in a fit of red-faced giggling, hands over their mouths, as if that could be effective in concealing their raucous joy.

John passed the stick he found in the rose garden to me. "Just look at this baby, Annabel."

"It's lovely," I said, pressing my finger onto the pointy end. We both sat staring at it.

"What was Frank's dad like?" I asked.

"His dad?"

"Yeah, Beth was telling me about his mom. What about his dad?"

"He died of a heart attack before Lily married Frank. He was a good man, who always tried to keep everyone happy. Frank turned out like him. Good hearted, with no trace of bitterness. But his mom, she spent her entire life bitter, up until the end. Up until Frank died. Then things changed."

Soon after Frank passed away, his mother became ill and was placed in a nursing home. Though few people believed her, she insisted that Frank came and visited her at 5:08 every day. He would stay exactly seven minutes, unless someone else was in the room. He would vanish if a nurse came in, and if anyone was there at arrival time, he would skip the visit that day. Vera always wished the visits could be longer, but they always brought dinner at 5:15. She would tell them she wanted to skip, but they insisted on bringing it, and unknowingly, ending Frank's visit. One day, she remembered how she used to trick Frank by resetting the clock. If she wanted him to go to bed early or turn off a video game or get ready for work faster, if she wanted him to exercise longer or do more homework, she set the clock back. She figured maybe, it would still work, even with the distance that now separated them in the space that fills the void between time and eternity.

It did. Frank came early.

He must have known she needed that time with him. Vera had begun to understand things she never had before, and she would tell Frank about them. She would tell him all the things she wished she could have known, all the things she wished she could do over. All the love she wished she would have been willing to give.

"You know who else visited Frank's mother every day?"

"Who?"

"Lily. Every day until the day she died. I was often the one to drive Lily to the hospital to visit her, so I became Frank's mother's confidant, and I can tell you, that woman served so much time in purgatory at the end of her life, I wouldn't be surprised if she didn't go straight to heaven, despite her many transgressions all her life. And there were many. Not everyone gets the chance that Beverly Greeley got, you know."

Though she herself would have never thought of it this way, my Grandma Bev got a second chance to love Lily the way Lily deserved. In Bev's dying days, she was able to give the things she never could when her body was whole. It was as if her heart became more functional as her body declined. And Lily was still around to receive that great gift that only a parent can give a child. Not that Bev was a bad parent in the earlier days. She just didn't recognize, in the day-to-day struggle of washing out underpants and forcing on a defiant child's shoes, that an invaluable gift had been bestowed on her. How many parents really do realize that at the time they are enduring it?

"And how do I, a young single guy with no children, have such an insight?" John pondered.

"Good question," I agreed. "How?"

"I have been schooled in the life of Lily. I have experienced her first hand and I have read all that Bev had to say on the topic of loving Lily and having Lily love her. And I'm sure I must see the world through a different lens because of it." He looked up into the sky and studied it for a minute. "Looks like Tasha's going to have a perfect wedding day. Weather report calls for more of the same tomorrow."

I pushed the stick into the ground with minimal effort. Typical Seattle soil. "A perfect, cloudless day."

⁖❂⁗

7

Love in the Trenches

The weather man was right. Tasha's wedding day was warm and breezy and drenched in the gold rays of summer. The kids were all flitting about the garden in their fancy clothes waiting for the wedding to start, tempting fate to deliver a grass stain or a ripped stocking, giving ulcers to all the adults who had spent hours choosing and altering little taffeta and lace dresses and hobbit-sized yet urbane tuxedos, pressing crisp white shirts and iron-willed cowlicks and adorning curls with baby's breath, rhinestone baubles and pearl fripperies. It could all be undone by a single misstep into a rosebush or by the untimely start of automatic sprinklers.

For some reason, maybe because I was standing around with nothing to do, it was decided that I should be the one to keep all the children calm and seated on the garden benches until it was time to go into the church.

Maybe I'm partial, but Beth's kids are, to me, the best endowed with personality. They have a sparkle about them, like they might leave a trail of pixie dust. They look you straight in the eye, a rare thing in their generation.

After playing a half dozen rounds of telephone and getting results such as "golden mayors eat kidneys," "trinkets are perfect for ginger," and "the end of the day is the meaning of glass," the game seemed to be getting a little old, and I feared losing some of them to the lure of all the things you can do on foot in a beautiful wide-open courtyard. I decided to engage them in conversation.

"What are you learning in school these days?"

"We are learning about the history of archeology," said an 11-year-old boy from Oscar's side of the family.

"What's that?" a boy of about seven asked.

"So, like for instance, how they once discovered a new dinosaur in Montana, I think it was? It wasn't like any other dinosaur. They named it Jane."

"Jane? How could it be called Jane?" Beth's four-year-old Lucy wanted to know. "T-Rexes are boys."

"Not all of them," said nine-year-old Leslie.

"Uh-huh," said Lucy

"That would be impossible," said a 13-year-old girl. "You can't have a species of all males."

"Hmmm," I mused. "Maybe that's how they became extinct."

"Well, first of all, Jane was not a T-Rex," said the 11-year-old. "Second, even though dinosaurs are ugly and awesomely epic, they can be females."

Father Fitz stopped in the courtyard to say hello to the kids, who upon seeing his car pull up, had all gotten off their benches, preparing to swarm him. He was much thinner than the last time I saw him. When I told him so, he told me he eats mostly salads and bikes at least three times a week to the gym, which is twelve miles from the rectory. He somehow remembered me by name.

Father Daniel was the last to arrive at the church. When he and Beth shook hands, I couldn't help but picture them as the couple they once were. They looked good together, if you discount the clerics. He is just about a head taller than she is, and they are both lean and beautiful. I would have thought they were meant for each other had I never seen Beth with Michael. Beth and Michael have a certain something between them that is not common to many romantic couples. It is a non-concrete, unquantifiable quality, like they were born for each other. Like there was a thought in someone's mind at the beginning of time that history should march toward the moment when their two paths crossed. I guess on the movie screen it would be called chemistry. In real life, I can only picture that when they first met, it was more like a reunion, that they had known each other before and had been looking for each other ever since, even though the memory of each other's faces had been lost somehow. I can't tell you exactly what I see in them, but I witnessed this moment between the two of them that told the entire story.

Miranda had fallen and skinned her knee and had run to her mother and then her father and then her mother again, accumulating hugs and sympathy, but not enough to stop the crying. "Owie, owie, owie, it hurts, it hurts it hurts!"

Without looking at each other, Beth and Michael opened their mouths at the same time and out came, in perfect harmony, some kind of song for healing boo boos on the knee. I don't remember the words, but I wish I did because it was very effective and I may need it someday.

ಙ⚜ಶ⚜ಙ⚜ಶ⚜ಙ⚜ಶ⚜ಙ⚜ಶ

I hadn't been to a Catholic Mass in recent memory, and I was looking forward to re-acquainting myself with the rituals and practices. Aside from my own Baptism when I was six months old, I've been only to weddings and funerals. I have always enjoyed them. Well, maybe enjoy is the wrong verb for funerals, but I found comfort in that lifting of the veil between heaven and earth that seems to take place inside a Cathedral.

Tasha has always wanted to be Catholic, though she didn't always know what Catholic was. She just knew it looked beautiful in the movie the Lovelys showed her when she was a small child and that she requested to watch every day for five weeks, completely memorizing every word of the "doe a deer song" and "goat song," as she called them, and donning Laura's half slip, from her armpits down, pretending to be Maria in her large elliptical wedding gown, floating down the aisle of the baroque Mondsee Cathedral toward her adoring Capt. Von

Trapp. Tasha and Oscar came into the Church, receiving their sacraments of initiation on Easter Vigil, 444 days before their wedding at St. James Cathedral in Seattle. You can guess what her dress looked like. We were all surprised she didn't insist on the highly-orchestrated version of *How Do You Solve a Problem Like Maria* as her entrance song. Maybe out of respect for liturgical norms, she chose *Canon in D*. Baby's breath intermingled with her long, cascading, curly red hair under a lace veil borrowed from Terry's wedding day.

ಬಿ೫ಛ೫ಬಿ೫ಛ೫ಬಿ೫ಛ೫ಬಿ೫ಛ೫ಬಿ೫ಛ

I was wondering who would give the homily. It turned out to be the elder priest, Father Fitz. I had never heard anyone say anything like this at a wedding. Actually, I don't think I've heard anyone say anything like this anywhere.

"The human experience is not for wimps. Being human means being heroic. None of us makes it through to the end without weathering the battle. That's why we need each other. Oscar and Tasha, you two are in the foxhole together. And you know what they say? There are no atheists there. People in the trenches, they need God and they need each other. And guess what? We are all in the trenches. And we all need to have each other's backs. Maybe if St. Paul were alive today, that's what he would have said to married couples. But back then, he said, 'husbands love your wives as Christ loved his Church.' We all know what Christ did for His Church. Look at the crucifix. It is just madness. He did what no one in their right mind would do. But that's love. Love is crazy like that."

Those words sting as I remember them now. I know which trenches he was talking about. I know where they are. I was there with Marty. And I regret that he was crazy, and I was not, and he and Bennie suffered because of my sanity.

After the wedding, I introduced myself to Father Danny and asked him if he would be going to the reception.

"I won't be able to come, unfortunately," he said. "I have a very packed calendar these days. But I wouldn't have missed this nuptial Mass for the world."

"Do you mind if I ask your opinion on something or are you pressed for time right now?"

"No, not at all. What's on your mind?"

"It's kind of a ridiculous question for a grown woman to have, but I came on this trip to find an answer, and I'm desperate. Beth told me you have a degree in psychology, so I thought I'd ask you."

"You want to know what true love is."

"Yes. How did you—"

"That's an easy one. You don't need a degree in psychology. You just need to look at the cross."

"To tell you the truth, I have never understood Catholics' fascination with the cross. It's not only an implement of torture, but the instrument by which the man they profess to love more than anything or anyone else in the world was killed."

"Oh, we're not merely fascinated with it. We venerate it."

"Yes. Veneration. How does that make sense?"

"How does God hanging on a cross make sense? The all good, all powerful, all loving God, killed by man."

"It doesn't."

"Right. Are you looking for good sense or are you looking for love? When you look at the cross, you will find one, but not the other. I'll bet you can guess which one."

I wasn't going to ask any more questions because Father Danny was going down a far different road from any route on my map, and I figured the answers would not be applicable or useful to me. Looking back on it now, I wish I had. There was no way of knowing back then that I would, indeed, need that information. How I wish I had it now, after all that has happened.

With the chicken dance well underway, Tasha had time to make the rounds and talk to the few guests who weren't standing in the circle in the middle of the dance floor flapping their wings. "I hear you may be next," she told me, as we sat together for a few minutes at my table.

"Oh, you heard that?"

"Yes. Is it not true?"

"I'm not sure yet. I'm supposed to give my boyfriend an answer. But everything in my life is so up in the air."

"Do you love him?"

"I do. I love him."

"Then, what more important thing is up in the air? Love is wonderful. I highly recommend it."

"Yes, most new brides do. I'll bet you're excited to start your life together."

"Feels more like a continuation, actually, than a start. We've been through a lot together already."

Tasha was Terry's first foster child. She left the Lovely home when she was a toddler to live with her maternal grandmother. When the grandmother passed away ten years later, it was fortunate that the social worker who had originally placed Tasha with the Lovelys happened to have returned to her same position just before Tasha re-entered the system at the age of twelve. The caseworker remembered how devastated the Lovelys were to let her go, so she called Terry. But the house was already full. The caseworker wanted to know if Terry wanted to shift one of her five foster kids to a different home to make room for Tasha since the home was only authorized for five. Terry had never lost her attachment to Tasha, but she could not bring herself to ask any of her current kids to leave, even though a couple of them had caused her a great deal of grief, most especially a 14-year-old boy named Oscar.

"Maybe there's a more suitable placement for Oscar elsewhere," the case worker said. "Not every kid thrives in every environment. You know that. You're a veteran. I don't have to tell you that."

"No," Terry said. "I can't give up on him. I can't ask him to leave. Who knows what that would do to him."

So it was decided that they would find another home for Tasha. About a week later, a couple materialized out of nowhere wanting to adopt a 13-year-old girl in Terry's care. The girl would go live with the couple as a foster child while adoption paperwork was being processed. This created an immediate opening in the Lovely home. Tasha had just unpacked her bags at another foster home, but that family understood when she told them she wanted to live with the Lovelys.

"It was actually Lily who first noticed that Oscar and I were in love," Tasha said. "We spent all our free time together. There was really nothing going on between us, you know. We were kind of like brother and sister. I mean, I guess I always had a bit of a crush on him. But we shared a lot of really heavy stuff. We would go up on the roof at night and talk for hours. But Lily said we were in love and then Frank started teasing us. Anyway, when Oscar turned eighteen, he left and we lost contact for awhile. He lived a pretty screwed up life for a while, even ended up in jail for DUI, had a whole string of trashy girlfriends and ended up somehow at a Christmas party kind of thing which was really like this reunion of all of Terry's foster kids. She throws one every year and for some reason, that year — this would have been three years ago — he came. We ended up back on the roof talking, just like old times. At one point, he told me that life pretty much sucked ever since he left Terry's and part of the reason is he missed the roof. He grabbed my hand and told me he hasn't been able to talk to anyone like he talks to me. He actually told me there were times he'd thought of killing himself, but then he'd imagine my face, pleading with him not to. He realized none of the girls he was with, even the one who had his baby, cared anything about him. When he got word of the reunion, he decided he should go and see if I was there, not for romantic reasons. But because he needed me. I was shocked. All my life, I always felt like a burden on someone. But Oscar actually needed me. It was an incredible thing."

"And he still needs you," I said.

"Yeah. And I need him. I know that's not a very romantic reason to fall in love and get married, but it is what it is."

"On the contrary, I think that's very romantic. You snatched him from the darkness and into the light of your embrace. And now he can't live without the light."

As I watched Tasha and Oscar's limo pull away, I imagined it was me and Logan, riding off to our lives together. I felt nothing.

Lucy grabbed me around the legs and buried her head in my coral silk skirt.

"What's the matter?" I bent down and put my arm around her. She was too red-faced to answer. "Are you going to miss Tasha?"

She nodded her head fiercely. Leslie and Miranda were standing by, looking gloomily at Lucy, feeling her pain. Feeling their own.

I hugged Lucy tighter. "She'll be back soon, Honey. Don't worry. She'll come play with you again soon."

"But that's a very big car. It can go a long way."

"Hey, how 'bout, if your Mommy says it's ok, we go home and set up a tent in the family room and get our favorite stuffed animals and pretend we're camping." I looked at Leslie and Miranda for approval.

"We don't have a tent."

"We'll make a tent. With blankets and sheets. When I was a kid, that used to be one of my favorite things to do on rainy days."

"But it's not raining today," Lucy pointed out.

"Yeah, but you're raining a little bit on the inside, aren't you?"

She nodded earnestly. "And some of it came out my eyes."

It was almost nine o'clock by the time we had set up camp, fed each of the stuffed animals imaginary hot dogs on imaginary sticks, sang a couple of campfire songs and played red light green light. If I was a male cousin, I would have told ghost stories and took turns shining the flashlight on each of our faces from the chin up to scare the stripes off each other. But I didn't want Beth and Michael to end up with frightened kids in their bed tonight after such a grueling forty-eight hours of activity.

I slipped off into the study to read *Pride & Prejudice* while Beth and Michael got the kids ready for bed, not planning to fall into a catnap. I awoke when I heard their five voices say, in near unison, except for the six-year-old who lagged a half-beat behind and the four-year-old who hurried a full syllable ahead, "in the name of the Father and the Son and the Holy Spirit. Amen."

I heard them pray for many things: the souls in Purgatory, their neighbor's cat who has cancer, their teacher's mother who has cancer, their family members near and far, for all sinners to stop sinning and go to heaven, for all field mice swiped by hawks to go to heaven, for peace in the Middle East and the whole world, for an end to abortion, for the safety of children, for old people in nursing homes, for the weather to be nice for Tasha's honeymoon, for Oscar and Tasha to have a happy life, for Oscar and Tasha to have lots of kids so there will be more kids in the family to play with. Michael prayed "in Thanksgiving for a wonderful wife, a best friend and devoted mother to my children" and that Oscar and Tasha would be as happy as Beth has made him through the years. This was met with a chorus of oohs and ahs, both sincere and sarcastic, and a clearly grateful "thank you, Honey" from Beth, who added her own prayer of Thanksgiving for her husband. Although the wall was between us, I felt compelled to join in the prayers, offering a silent petition to a God I had not spoken to for quite some time: that I would make the right decisions and not mess up my life. Beth announced that it was now officially bedtime, which made everyone suddenly thirsty again. A flurry of activity advanced into the kitchen. Ice dropped into glasses, water ran and a cacophony of voices registered questions, comments, complaints and requests in last-ditch maneuvers to delay bedtime. Someone, of course, had to pee again, and then someone else had to pee too. And then there was a renewed thirst, I guess from that arduous trip to the bathroom. So, more ice and more water. And more comments.

"It will be cool when grandma and grandpa die," said Miranda.

"Cool?" Leslie was shocked.

"Yeah, then they will be angels. And they'll be able to fly around. And they will be able to talk to all the saints."

"I'm going to be shy to talk to the saints," said Lucy, who is four.

"No, you won't be shy," Beth said.

"But I am shy. And I'll still be shy in Heaven."

"But you won't be shy to talk to the saints," Beth reiterated. "When you see them, you'll realize you've known them all your life. They are like our big brothers and big sisters and you will recognize them right away and you will want to just run and give them big hugs and talk to them all about their lives and all about your life."

"But right now, it's time for bed," their father said. He agreed to lay down with them if they agreed to play the quiet game.

I was refreshed from my nap and wandered out into the kitchen when all was quiet.

"Would you like some tea, Annabel?" Beth asked, stacking crusted over breakfast plates into the dishwasher.

"No, thanks. I'm fine. You want me to scrub those? They might not come out clean."

"No, I'll scrub them after they come out if they need it. Might as well see what the dishwasher can do."

"Do you want me to fold up the tents and put them back in the linen cabinet?"

"No, I promised the girls they would still be there

tomorrow so they could play some more. They really enjoyed that."

"Me too." I picked up a dish rag from behind the faucet and began wiping the counters. "I'm not going to want to go home. I've got it too good here."

"I'm sure the girls wouldn't mind that at all."

"They are sweet. I wish life could stay that simple."

"Me too." She glanced into my face. "It's gotten pretty complicated for you, huh?"

"Yeah. Only Brad Beauchamp could bring such angst into my life."

"Oh, the egg eliminator. Well, I don't know him very well, obviously, but I don't like him."

"How come?"

"He's a wimp."

"What makes you say that?"

"He can't deal with any imperfections. I can't imagine being married to someone like that."

"No, I don't think he's like that. I never felt like I had to be perfect to be with him."

"That's because you are nearly perfect. What more could he ask for in a woman than what you've got to offer? But what if some day you don't have so much to offer? What if, God forbid, you're in a car accident some day and you're paralyzed or brain injured? Then what?"

"You think he won't take care of me?"

"I think he'll walk. Or worse yet, try to get them to pull the plug."

"How do you glean all this information on someone you've never even met?"

"Look what he's doing for his life's work. Trying to create a perfect race."

"Trying to alleviate unnecessary human suffering."

"If you're trying to alleviate unnecessary suffering, there's one sure way to do it, and it has nothing to do with the genetic engineering of humans. The key word you use there is 'unnecessary.' Suffering is a part of life. Some of it is quite necessary. The unnecessary variety is the one brought on by your own self. If there is one thing I would tell young people, it would be to be careful about the mistakes you make when you are young. Everyone makes them, but there are some that do irreparable harm and you live every day of your life wishing you could have those moments back. You would die right then and there rather than hurt those people again. Now *that* is suffering."

At the time, I couldn't think of any moments in my life like that. I had no way of knowing that within a matter of weeks, I would know exactly what Beth was talking about and that I would be happy to have the earth swallow me up.

"So," Beth continued, "at that point you have two options: seek mercy or let the regret consume you. I've seen what the latter looks like. I've seen that regret doesn't go away, no matter how many years pass. Actually it just gets uglier and uglier and checks itself right into the nursing home with you at the end of your life."

"One more reason to dread growing old."

"Well, there's the right way to do it and the wrong way. And speaking of the wrong way, has your father ever mentioned Jolene?"

"No. I don't think so."

"She's our biological grandmother. Your father's mother and my mother's mother."

"And Lily's?"

"No, not Lily."

"Wait, am I biologically related to Lily?"

"No. And neither am I."

"But you and I are related."

"Yes. My mother and your father are biological siblings, born to Jolene and adopted by a woman named Jennifer Eagan, who is Lily's biological mother, but died and left all her kids to her sister, Bev. So Lily is your father's and my mother's adoptive sister."

"Does your mom have contact with Jolene?"

"No, but I do."

"What is she like?"

"Oh, that's an impossible question to answer. There are no words to describe Jo. You have to just experience her firsthand. You can read some of her letters if you want." She went to a kitchen cabinet and took out a thick brown envelope. "Maybe, after you read these, you could tell me if I should show them to my mother. I haven't decided if I should. She doesn't know we've been corresponding."

"Would she be upset?"

"I don't think so. She has no interest in Jo. There's a long ancient history of hurt there, but my mother certainly doesn't dwell on it. There is no animosity there, she just doesn't see Jolene as relevant to her past or her future."

Beth handed me the envelope. I opened the flap, looked inside and saw a number of white envelopes, all of which had been opened along the edge, revealing folded lined, yellow notebook paper. "I'll look at these tonight and give them back in the morning."

"Not recommended bedtime reading. You'll have nightmares."

"That bad, huh?"

"Read them in the daylight."

I closed the envelope and put it with my purse on the couch. I picked up a picture on the side table and studied it. "Where was this taken?"

"At the animal clinic where Lily used to work with me. That's Pepper. That dog could actually talk. You know, without consonants, except R's. But still. Lily could understand every word he said."

I chuckled. "Why did Lily seem to have life all figured out. It's like she knew something the rest of us don't. She didn't labor over finding the answers to things. The answers just seemed to be there. At least, that's how I've always viewed her. I don't know if that's accurate."

"Yes, that's how it was with Lily."

"How did she do that?"

"Well, it probably has something to do with the central answer to all of life's questions."

"Please share. I'd love to know."

"Love."

"Love?"

"Yes, according to my mother, love is the answer to every question. Lily knew that and was able to incorporate it perfectly into her life because she knew love in its perfected state."

'And how was she able to know that?"

"I don't know. Maybe that's what the extra stuff on the twenty-first chromosome is all about. Maybe it gives the person a greater capacity to love. You're the geneticist. Does that make any sense?"

"Scientifically, no. But screw science. I like your theory."

ঔৠ৵

8

The Gift of Knots

I ignored Beth's advice, and that night I lay in bed and read Jolene's letters.

Dear Beth,

I know you think I should tell your mother I love her or something like that. But I don't see what good that would do. It doesn't change what happened. Anyway, it seems heartless to do that to her. What's she going to say — I love you too. No big deal you abandoned me? I know what I'd say to my father if he would have ever had the nerve to say that to me. I won't write it down. It's not fit to print, as they say. What I'd do to him isn't either.

Maybe you can come visit me. It's been a long time since I've had a visitor.

Take care,

Jo

Dear Beth,

I have to be honest with you. I don't know what answer to give you. You're asking me to feel something and know what it is I'm feeling. I am not used to doing either of those things. All I can tell you is I'm a lonely old lady who wishes I had loved my children. Wishes I could have. But I'm not expecting anything to change now. It didn't in the first 83 years of my life. It won't now. I guess you'd need to ask a shrink to find out why.

They have started to put up all the gold tinsel around

here, so I guess it's that cheerful time of year again. Still stinks like nobody's business.

Send me the size of your baby. They're going to shuttle us to the mall to go Christmas shopping, and I'd like to get her something.

Be nice to have a visit.

Take care,

Jo

Dear Beth,

There is an old priest who lives here. I never paid him any attention. Actually, he always kind of annoyed me. He makes rosaries by knotting string and goes around giving them to everybody. Kind of insensitive, if you ask me. Most of the people here aren't even Catholic. But they all smile and take them as if they know what to do with them. I have three in my sock drawer. It doesn't take much to make these people happy around here. Someone could give them a paper clip and they'd accept it like it was gold. Anyway, your Father Tomas "introduced" me to this priest awhile ago, meaning he gave him an assignment. So I have turned into his little project. I know what you're thinking. More like a very big project. Anyway, we play checkers together every Wednesday afternoon. Good looking guy for ninety-seven.

I been thinking about what you said. I don't agree, but I want you to know I've been thinking about it. I don't expect anyone to understand me. No one has walked in my shoes. I know you don't understand me. But you don't judge me either. So we can be friends. We are friends, aren't we? Is that what you would call us?

How is your mother?

Take care,

Jo

Dear Beth,

Did I tell you about my priest "friend"? This is a picture

he drew of me. I asked him to draw an extra so I could send you one. He drew it exactly the same as the first time. What do you think? Does it look like me? No one around here ever knew he could draw. Someone came by and brought him some paper and pens for his birthday and now he's been drawing everybody. Much better idea than the rosaries.

Thank you for your letter. It had been a long time since I heard from you. It gets pretty lonely here. Actually it's hell. Except it's not eternal. We're all waiting to "move on." Otherwise known as dying. So a letter can take your mind off that for a minute or two. Tell your mother I'd like to hear from her sometime. I talked to her on the phone for a few minutes the other day. She seemed distracted. I think she's waiting for something to change. It's not going to. At this stage of the game, nothing much changes.

Take care,
Jo

Stapled behind the letter was a caricature. Large round eyes encircled by a multitude of bags and folds. An unlit cigarette propped casually in between her lips. It was signed on the lower right with a "DdL"

Dear Beth,
Since you didn't send me your girl's size, I am sending something "one size fits all." This is one of the rosaries my priest friend made, since I know you are Catholic. He blessed it, so I guess that makes it special somehow. He wanted to know her name, but I forgot.

Take care,
Jo

Dear Beth,
I knew there was a reason why you and me get along so well. You are right. If it wasn't for the drugs, everything would have been different. You are lucky you got off when you did.

You don't want to end up like me at the end of your life. Or even in the middle.

My priest friend taught me how to say the Hail Mary prayer. Probably knows I need the "pray for us sinners" part. I had him pegged wrong in the beginning. He really isn't annoying. I am actually calling him "Father" now. I hated the last man I called that. But this one's not too bad.

Maybe you and your mother can come out for a visit sometime.

Take care,
Jo

Dear Beth,

Your mother wrote to me. Don't know exactly why. Her letter was all about that foster child of hers — a 14-year-old girl who was pregnant with her stepfather's baby. I don't know why she wanted to tell me about it. I guess maybe she figured misery loves company. She's trying to talk her out of getting rid of it. I don't know how she can expect that poor girl to carry her rapist's baby. Try to talk some sense into your mother, Beth, before she ends up laying a guilt trip on that girl when none of this is her fault.

Take care,
Jo

Dear Beth,

My priest friend told me he used to be rich. For about 48 hours. He inherited billions and then gave it away. I don't know whether to believe him or not. I never thought he had dementia, but maybe he does. I can't imagine anyone giving away that much money. Actually, I can't imagine anyone giving away all the money they have, no matter how much it is. But he did, apparently. I've been poor all my life, and I can tell you, poverty sucks. If I ever got some money, I can think of a lot of things I would do with it. First, I'd give ten percent to charity. I know what it's like to be hungry. I would give it to the food bank. I heard somewhere that people get back ten times what they give. No wonder I never got nothing. I've never had nothing to give. But if I had some money, I would buy a big house on a hill with lots for grass and trees around it. And I'd get me some horses. Some really nice quarter horses. And I'd ride through the trees all day long. I got to go to summer camp once and ride a horse. Was probably the best week of my life. Getting away from home was the best thing about it. I couldn't figure out why all the other kids were homesick. I dreaded going home from the second I got on the bus. About a week into it, I bled all over the tent floor. I told my tent mates I was having a bad period. I was actually having a miscarriage. At least I didn't have to do anything to get rid of that one. It just happened naturally. If miscarrying your father's baby could ever be called "natural."

Well, listen, my hand is beginning to ache here, I've written so much.

Take care of yourself,
Jo

Dear Beth,

Sure would be nice to see you for a visit. If I'm remembering right, tomorrow is my birthday. I'm sure they'll have a cupcake for me with a candle to blow out. Not sure there's much to celebrate unless of course they are aiming to celebrate the end of a crummy life. They allow everyone who is having a birthday to stand up and tell something about each decade of their lives. I'll probably just ask to skip the middle eight decades. I was born and now I'm dying. The end. And I can't say as I'm too broken up about that. My priest friend says every life is worth living. He's never gotten a tour of mine. You could tell him, Beth. You probably know more about my life than any other living soul.

Well, wish me a happy birthday and maybe I'll see you sometime soon.

Take care,
Jo

I awoke the next morning with the letters lying by my side. If they make anything clear, it is that human suffering can never be alleviated. There is no vaccine to prevent the conception of people like Jolene, whose genes are probably perfectly typical, but whose life has consisted of little else but misery due to what would seem to be the transgressions of her father and her own bitter response. I dare say those two people caused and wallowed in untold grief, and there is not, to my knowledge, any gene that predicts a person's disregard for the damage they do to others.

The house was quiet. Michael had taken the girls to the zoo for a zookeeper class Leslie had won for herself and her siblings by entering a drawing contest. I was exhausted and foggy headed, but the smell of toast and coffee and grilled butter drew me to the kitchen. It also made me miss home. Home as in my parent's house, not my own. I never awake to those kinds of aromas in my house. That's one of the problems of living alone. I have to say, I look forward to the day when my house is full. Of course, it will probably be me creating those morning aromas, except for maybe on weekends. From what I can tell, men don't cook breakfast on weekdays, though they will occasionally cook dinner. Logan is fairly handy in the kitchen. He had to learn to fend for himself as a kid, since his mother died young. Brad is a different story. He still goes over to his mother's house to eat, probably sixty percent of his meals.

I laid the package of Jolene's letters on the kitchen desk. "Interesting read," I told Beth as I watched her make a sausage and mushroom omelet. "What ever happened to that 14-year-old girl? The one your mom wrote Jolene about."

"She had her baby," Beth said, maneuvering a spatula under the semi-circle of eggs. "And I named her Leslie."

"I had a feeling. What made her decide to have the baby?"

"I told her there's a huge, long line of people waiting to be parents. She asked me if I would adopt her baby. I honestly

80

felt several moments of guilt at the thought of cutting that line. But then I realized all of this was no accident and that this baby must have been meant to be mine. And I can tell you, the older she gets, the more I know this to be true."

"It's funny. She really looks like you."

"Poor kid."

"Are you unable to have children of your own?"

"Well, Lucy and Miranda and Leslie are my own. But if you mean biological children, yes. None have come to us. For awhile, I just figured it was God's plan for us to be childless. I didn't feel worthy to stand in that long line waiting for a baby to adopt. So I told God, if He dropped a baby in our laps, we would be delighted. But short of that, we would take it as a sign that we are being called to something besides parenthood."

"And then came Miranda and Lucy."

"Yes. Same mother, different fathers. Also, dropped in our laps."

"But you would recommend it?"

"What?"

"Marriage and parenthood."

"Yes, highly. On most days. Are you considering it?"

"Yes, considering it, I suppose. Along with other big changes."

"Oh, the job offer."

"Yes."

"Wow. I just can't picture it. No more Lilys in the world. That would be tough."

"You know we wouldn't be eliminating them after they are conceived, right?" A couple of bagels popped up in the toaster. "They would just never be conceived."

"So an imperfect person would never have the chance of making it into the world."

"What chance does any one person have anyway? A woman is born with a million eggs."

"But only the people without disabilities will be spared."

"Well, they're not people yet. An egg is nothing more

than a genetic code. I don't see how that's discrimination against any person when an egg is not a person."

"What you say makes sense from a scientific point of view. I guess I just don't want to imagine a world without Lilys. Without Franks."

"I know. I have a tough time with that too."

As I spread cream cheese on the bagels, another argument came to me. "So we should keep disabled people around because they enrich our lives. Is that what we're saying?"

"No. We should keep disabled people around because they were meant to have life every bit as much as the rest of us who ended up, against all odds, being conceived."

"And we're not just being selfish, then, wanting to keep them around?"

"Ask any person with Down syndrome if they would rather not have been born. What do you think they will say?"

I looked at the half bagel I decided would be mine and smoothed out the cream cheese along the edges with my fingers.

"You know what they will say," Beth said, sipping her coffee.

I licked my finger and bit into the bagel. "They will say, 'Hey, lady, keep your hands off our eggs and find yourself another job.'"

"And marry that guy that you love."

"But there are tremendous odds against any one of us getting here in the first place. What's the big deal about eliminating some eggs that had a highly, highly slim chance of ever contributing to creation?"

"I don't know, but I'm sure someone smarter than me could tell you what the big deal is. Look, you can ask me, you can ask your mom and dad, you can ask someone with Down syndrome, you can ask Gandhi. But the real question is not what any of us think. The question is, 'what does God think?'"

"What does God think."

"I've heard it said that the chances of being born are the same odds as 2.5 million people rolling a trillion-sided dice and all coming up with the same number. Incredible odds, unbelievable odds, had to be overcome to get any one of us here. If even one of our numerous generations of ancestors had not made it to child-bearing years, we would not be here. So there must be a reason for each person that exists. Who are we to take that person out of the running by obliterating his or her egg?"

I neglected to ask Beth how one goes about asking God what He thinks.

"And speaking of eggs," Beth said turning off the stove, "I think this omelet is done."

"Looks great."

"So, what did you think," she asked, sliding the eggs onto a plate, "of our Grandma Jo?"

"Depressing." I took two orange napkins from the wrought iron rooster napkin holder, folded them into an obtuse triangle and put them on opposite ends of the oval table. "And yet, not completely devoid of hope."

"Do you think I should show them to my mom?"

"What are the pros and cons?"

"Well, those letters were written quite a while ago. Jolene hasn't written in awhile. I've spoken to her on the phone, but she is really not well, and I know she'd like to see my mom again before she dies. Your dad too, I'm sure."

"Well, I don't think that's ever going to happen. But as far as your mom goes, I'm not sure those letters are going to give her any kind of warm fuzzies that would send her rushing to board a flight to go visit this woman."

"You wouldn't think so," said Beth, placing forks on top the napkins. "Only if you could see how far she's come. I know my mother would see a difference in the woman she spent a half hour with almost a decade ago and the one who writes these letters."

"She visited her before?"

We sat, and Beth closed her eyes for several seconds and made the sign of the cross before picking up her fork. "She happened to be in California where Jolene's nursing home is."

"So those letters represent the new and improved Jolene?"

"Yes, sadly," she said taking a bite of omelet. "But I think my mother had a lot to do with the improvement, and I think it would do her good to see it. Do we need salt?"

"No, this tastes great. Why do people have to get to the end of their lives to figure things out?"

"I guess aging is kind of the slow chipping away at all the things that keep us from doing the one thing we were created to do." The second round of bagels popped up.

"Love."

"Yes. My mother would be proud of you." Beth raised a glass of orange juice to toast my wisdom. "Love it is."

ಖ෴ಞ෴ಖ෴෴ಖ෴෴෴ಖ෴෴

Miami International gives you your choice of vending machines. One offers coffee, tea and hot cocoa. The other dispenses soda and the third has juices and water. As a kid, I was always fascinated by the coffee vending machines — how the cup comes down first, then the coffee. And then cream if you've chosen it. I have to admit, I am still a bit fascinated with it, and I have to tell myself not to factor that process into my decision. I have to focus on what I truly want to drink. Actually, I truly want coffee. I will always choose coffee if I base my choice on what I truly want. But I choose orange juice in honor of Beth's toast and in hopes I can come to understand exactly what it was we were toasting. Plus, I might need some vitamin C. I am not feeling all that well. I find a seat near the window where I can watch the planes take off. A dad with a couple of cranky young children sits opposite me. Lying at their feet, each of the kids has a backpack with some gender-appropriate cartoon character I don't recognize, reminding me I am getting too old to keep up with pop culture. The little girl, arms crossed, slouching, is swinging her feet. Both of her shoe laces are untied, and I am fixated on them, so that all I can think about is my desire for them to be tied.

Lily went the first thirty-eight years of her life without tying her shoe. Not for want of people trying to teach her. Eventually, Bev decided the world had enough Velcro to make the art of shoe tying optional, if not obsolete.

But then Frank came along. Inside the span of a ten-minute Lesson, he had Lily tying a ribbon in her hair. He told her she would look pretty that way and that was all the motivation she needed to put her failures behind her and make the squirrel run around the tree and jump into the hole.

It was never determined whether Frank had a gift of knots or whether it was the many hours he spent with his older brother, an Eagle Scout. But one thing is for certain, Frank was proficient with string. He once even made a Macramé chair. It took him seven weeks. When it was done, he moved his wooden chair at the dining room table out and replaced it with that one. For three years, that's where he sat for games of cards, rounds of homework and Lego construction. But not for consuming food.

For the majority of his life, Frank would stand up when he ate. People assumed it was a Down syndrome thing. It was actually a Stillwell thing. His whole family did it. Nobody sat at the table to eat. The Stillwell tables were used for many things (writing grocery lists, unpacking backpacks, constructing 1,000-piece puzzles, laptop web browsing, folding laundry). But not for food. The Stillwells were counter grazers. It was as if sitting might slow the process of eating. They ate with loins girded and sandals on their feet, as if it was the Passover and they were waiting for their release from some kind of bondage.

Few people in Lily's family ever ate at the table either. They slouched on sofas, feet propped on the coffee table, plates of food in their hands, watching old movies and vintage sit-coms. There were, of course, exceptions to this venue. If soup or spaghetti was on the menu, or if there was company, the Lovelys ate in chairs, seated at the dining table.

When Frank and Lily got married, people took bets on which eating style would prevail in the newlywed home. Most people thought the couch would win out over the counter. First, it is, of course, more comfortable. Second, Lily had the stronger personality. Not that she always got her way or even demanded it. And not that she was unwilling to serve Frank, just as he served her. It was simply that Lily belonged to that class of human beings known as leaders, and Frank belonged to the one known as followers. And that was more than fine with Frank. Following Lily was fun. She was a cruise director, not a dictator. And as with the majority of cruises, the food was always plentiful.

Lily always kept the basics (frozen pizza and Wonder Bread) well stocked, but since she worked at a grocery store, she shopped for dinner ingredients every day. Lily started her marriage with a solid repertoire of dishes and added more as she learned of Frank's favorites. She did most of the cooking, except on special occasions, like on her birthday, or when she was feeling too tired. On those occasions, Frank cooked, and the dog ate well. Lily would have never told Frank his cooking was unfit for human consumption, so she would sneak bits at a time under the couch, where Snowball eagerly snapped it up — another advantage to eating on the couch and not at the counter.

ↄ✿Ↄ

9

Splitting Black & Whites

I try to balance my vending machine coffee on the arm of my chair, but the arm is a little too skinny, and I decide it's too risky. I have left coffee stains a number of places in the world, but I want to spare Miami International. I reposition my purse to make room for the cup on the flattest part of the chair seat next to me. My purse jumps off the chair and its contents spill. It looks like someone dumped out a trashcan right in the middle of the airport terminal. It's been too long since I cleaned out my purse.

The last time, actually, was on Tuesday, June 22. The second and fourth Tuesdays of the month is clean out my purse day, according to my mother's schedule. Which is good because I had just returned from Tasha's wedding, and a purse always needs a cleaning out after a trip. There are always a number of gum wrappers shoved in there when no trash receptacle can be found or when you're too lazy to cross the street to get to one. There are baggage check tabs and extra hair bands. Unopened flight peanuts saved for a time when your stomach isn't so unsettled.

And there was this: a musician's card. So, I picked up the phone.

"Hi, Marty, this is Annabel. I met you at the reception for the new facility for the disabled. Do you remember?"

"Sure, I remember. How are you?"

"I'm fine, and you?"

"Great."

87

"I just pulled your card out of my purse and I thought I should call and tell you that I went to a wedding this weekend in Seattle and I thought of you."

"Really?" He sounded exceedingly happy about this.

"The musician there wrote a song specifically for the couple getting married — you know, about how they met, the memories they've shared."

"Wow. That's neat."

"Yeah, and I was talking to him afterward and he told me that he is so booked now since he's been doing that, he had to quit his day job. He is able to support his family of four kids on just weddings. So, I thought maybe I'd just pass that idea along to you. Maybe it will work for you too."

"That's a great idea. But I wouldn't want to quit my day job, which is actually a day and night job. I love it too much. Music is my dessert, and if I made it part of my main course, it might turn into broccoli. But writing songs for couples — that sounds fun."

"Great. Well, that's what I wanted to pass along to you."

"Thank you. Thank you so much. I can't believe how thoughtful that is. Thank you so much."

"Sure."

"If you'd like, I'll try it out on you and your fiancé. On the house, of course."

"Oh, that's very nice. But you don't have to do that."

"I'd like to. Really. If you don't mind being my guinea pig."

"No, not at all. The only thing is, to tell you the truth, I'm still not sure there's going to be a wedding."

"Really? Well, whenever you're ready, just let me know."

"OK, sounds good."

"I'm going out of town for a few weeks, but I'll be back the end of July."

"OK. Maybe I'll call you. Have a safe vacation."

"Thank you. But it's not really a vacation. I'm going on a

mission."

"Really? Where?"

"Jamaica."

"Sounds real tough."

"It is actually. It's not exactly a cocktail-sipping, ukulele-playing kind of trip."

"What will you do there?"

"There are a lot of very poor people there, and people who are extremely sick and have no one to care for them. If it wasn't for the mission house, they would be literally lying in the street dying. I go there once a year to help out."

"They give you the time off work?"

"I get four weeks of vacation a year. I use three of them for the Missionaries of Joy."

"What do you do with the fourth?"

"I usually just clean my garage and play my music. Some years, if I can afford it, I'll go to the Cape, stay in a bed and breakfast and write some songs."

"Cape Cod?"

"Yeah. It's one of my favorite places on earth. Not that I've been too many places on earth."

"The Cape is beautiful."

"But not nearly as beautiful as the Kingston ghetto."

"You're employing irony, right?"

"No, I don't think so. Not sure what that means."

"You're being sarcastic."

"No, I'm serious."

"Really? How is a ghetto beautiful?"

"You'd have to experience Kingston to know what I'm talking about. But the poor and the sick are very, very beautiful."

"Hmmm."

"I know it sounds strange. I'd like to be able to explain it. But you just really have to be there to understand."

"Maybe someday I'll go."

"Really? You would be interested in going?"

"Sure."

"Well, actually a couple scheduled to go had to cancel because they got sick. So the mission could use an extra hand."

"Oh, you mean now?"

"Well, not now. Friday."

"Oh, I think I'd have to prepare. I can't just, you know, fly off to Jamaica."

"True. True. Well, maybe someday."

"Yeah, someday. I'd like to. Someday."

ஐ௯ஜ௯ஐ௯ஜ௯ஐ௯ஜ௯ஐ௯ஜ௯ஐ

Logan has had the same plug-in air freshener since I've known him and it permeates his house and everything in it, so that when he lends you a book, you can smell midnight pomegranate on its pages, even after you've borrowed it for more than a month. I wish I could tell you if it smells the way a midnight pomegranate ought to, but I don't have a point of reference for that, and I don't know who would. It's a pleasant aroma, for sure, but I would never choose it for my home because every time I smell it, my mind leaves whatever item of business was before it and goes off on a tangent of contemplation: what focus group or chemist or product engineer or advertising executive came up with that name for that smell — deep and sweet and exotic. Like eating a pomegranate at midnight, I guess. Or picking one? Or planting one?

Logan suggested we sit by his fire pit and share a bottle of wine so I could tell him all about Tasha's wedding, most likely in hopes that it would get me thinking about ours. He put a big Mexican blanket around my shoulders. There was a bit of cool dampness in the air, and I was impressed that he remembered I am easily chilled.

"An old friend has asked me to join him in a new project," I told him as we settled in together on soft all-weather cushions.

"Really? What is the project?"

"It's a vaccine to eliminate a number of birth defects."

90

"Sounds exciting. Are you going to take it?"

"I don't know."

"What's the pay?"

"I don't know. I'm sure it is very lucrative."

"Long hours?"

"Probably."

"Hmm. You'll have to weigh all that. See if it's worth it."

"Well, it's ground-breaking work. I doubt there would be anything in my field that would be more important than this in my lifetime. It is huge."

"Sounds great. I'm proud of you, Honey. If you decide to take it. And even if you don't. To be offered something like this — you must feel honored. Who would you be working with? Who's your friend?"

"Brad Beauchamp."

"Brad Beauchamp? Do I know him?"

"I don't think so."

"How do you know him?"

"We dated."

"Were you serious?"

"Yes, And no."

"What does that mean?"

"I was. He wasn't."

"How long did you date?"

"Three or four years."

"Four years?!"

"Mostly during graduate studies."

"Well, how's that going to be for you? Working with an old lover?"

"I don't know. To tell you the truth, that's part of what's holding me back."

"Oh, I'm glad you feel that way. Well, as long as you no longer have feelings for him..."

I stared at the fire.

"Do you still have feelings for him?"

"I don't think so."

"Hmmm. That's a big yes."

"If we were married and you didn't want me to take the job, I wouldn't."

"I'm not saying that. You will have to make that decision. I trust you. Whatever you decide. You can't let an important career move pass you up just because of an old boyfriend."

"That's very understanding of you."

"I'm an understanding guy. I'm telling you, Anna, you'll not find a more accommodating fellow. All I wish for is your happiness."

"That's sweet. Thank you."

He moved my chin toward his face and gave me a long kiss and then settled back into the cushions, resting his head on the back of the sofa, staring up into the stars.

"When do you have to make the decision?"

"Soon." I threw a leaf into the fire and watched the flames devour it.

"And have you made your decision about us?"

"Not yet. I'm sorry."

"Take your time, Anna. I am here waiting for you." He took a drink of wine.

I threw in another leaf. "Did you know my mother nearly aborted me?"

"What? Why?"

"They told her I would be born with Down syndrome."

It was all he could do to keep the wine from spewing from his mouth as a shocked laughter overtook him. "Well, there couldn't have been a more mistaken diagnosis. Your poor mother, having to go through that. Having to worry for all those months."

"She came very close to terminating the pregnancy. Do you know why she decided to keep me?"

"Why?"

"Aunt Lily. I have an aunt with Down syndrome."

"Really? You never told me that."

"I haven't?" This shocked me. "I'm surprised. I talk about Lily all the time. Well, maybe I just think about her all the time."

"I wish you would think about me all the time, Anna." He kissed me again. "What can I do to become your one obsession?"

I smiled and stroked his hair. "I don't know, Logan. I just don't know. Any sane woman would be crazy about you."

He smiled and sipped his wine. "So, is Down syndrome hereditary? I mean does it run in families?"

"Relax, Logan. Lily is not my biological aunt. My father was adopted. And to answer your question, no. The vast majority of Down syndrome cases are not hereditary. So our children would, of course, be perfect. Just like you."

ಬ⚹ಏ⚹ಬ⚹ಏ⚹ಬ⚹ಏ⚹ಬ⚹ಏ

Upon learning I had returned from the wedding in Seattle, Brad wanted to go grab a cup of coffee and some black and whites. It was our usual breakfast in college, after a long night of studying. I had never had a black and white before I moved away to college. The coffee shop in the student union sold them. They were huge, like the size of a dessert plate, and the first time we got one, we split it. For some reason, Brad split it along the line where the white and the brown frostings meet, making me choose which one I wanted. Actually I wanted both. I always wondered why he didn't split it the other way and allow us each a little lemon and a little chocolate. I was going to suggest that the next time, but that was the best cookie either one of us had ever had (I got the chocolate half) so we always got our own after that.

We'd be there on the couch together in the student union, sharing ear buds, anatomy notes and physiology texts, Brad rubbing my neck in between chapters, me talking about how great it will be to someday have all this behind us and enjoy our

93

lives together in our shared field. I would feel physically exhausted from waking up so early to try to cram for an exam, and then a single kiss from him would renew my strength.

Sitting there at Shilo's Cafe, years later, with our enormous cookies in front of us, I wished he would kiss me. I wanted to see if it was still the same for us. I wondered if I would feel guilty. How would I tell Logan? I would have to tell him or else resign myself to complete hypocrisy. This scenario was looking strangely familiar. I guess I finally understood how it could happen, how Brad could fall for his ex-girlfriend even while seeing me.

After our graduate studies at University of Oxford, I wanted to live in the UK awhile. Brad wanted to move back to his home state, so I followed him to Boston. It's a strange thought that he is actually the one who led me to Logan. Then to Marty. And Bennie. How I wish now I had never followed Brad.

"So," he said, pressing his finger on the crumbs on his plate and bringing them to his mouth, "how was Seattle?"

"Fine. Weather was nice. It was a beautiful wedding. I got to spend time with my second cousins and other assorted cute kids."

"Who, again, was getting married?"

"A couple of my aunt's foster children."

"Oh, nice." He picked up his half-empty coffee cup, looked inside and set it back down. "So, did you have some time to think?"

"A little bit."

We sat on tall stools at a long skinny table — more like a bar — that ran the entire width of a huge picture window overlooking Commonwealth Avenue.

"And?" he prompted.

"I don't know what to think."

"Why not?"

"I don't know. It's like I lack the ability to make decisions right now."

"Does this help?" He moved his lips toward mine, and I

turned away, pretending that something caught my attention inside a car that was pulling up outside the window. Brad also pretended to be interested in the car. I felt embarrassed for him for having to pretend he hadn't been rejected. I had been there before.

And then, suddenly, I actually was interested in what was going on outside the window. An elderly man, who could no longer lift his feet off the ground, scuffed from the driver's side around to the trunk, slowly lifted a walker out and set it up, pushed it to the passenger side and opened the door. He reached in, took his wife's hand and then gripped gently onto her arm to guide her to the walker. I don't think I had ever seen anyone so bent as she was, but she was beautiful. Her hair was fixed in short hair-sprayed blonde curls and I could see, from even my vantage point, her bright red fingernail polish. She couldn't look her husband in the eye, because she could look at nothing but the ground, so don't ask me how I knew that she smiled at him. Maybe because his eyes softened when she did. And at this moment, don't ask me why, I knew that my life was about to take a new direction. I had to find what those two people had found, maybe forty years ago, maybe fifty. Or maybe just yesterday.

ಬ✼ಐ

10

The Pit

I am quite sure there were absolutely no shocks on that rattling, rickety bus. My motion sickness was kicking in. We were in the second seat to the last of the *Royal Express.* Every small and large bump slammed my bottom onto the hard seat, jarring my vertebrae closer together. I feared that by the time I got there, my spine would be one long, fused, solid bone. My mother's voice told me to find a mint to settle my stomach, so I dug into my purse for a Tic Tac. It reminded me of Logan's lips. The man is addicted to Tic Tacs. I imagine that someone must have once told him he had bad breath and he, right then and there, resolved to spend the rest of his life with a mint in his mouth.

It was well past time to call him now. I thought it unkind to put it off any longer. I also knew he wouldn't understand what I was doing. I couldn't blame him. I didn't really understand it either. If anybody would have told me the week prior that I would be there in that place, I would have said they were crazy. But there I was, and I was going to have to try to explain it without sounding like a crazy person myself.

"Hello?"

"Hi, Logan."

"Anna, how are you?"

"I am well."

"What are you doing? Where are you?"

"I'm in Kingston."

"Kingston? Jamaica?

"Yes. Jamaica. Mon."

What are you talking about? How could you be in Jamaica?"

"It's a long story."

"Are you alone?"

"No. I have a friend with me."

"Who?"

"Marty."

I glanced at Marty when I said this and he gave me a quick smile and returned his eyes to the window.

"Marty? Who's Marty?"

"A friend. Just a friend." Marty kept looking out the window as if he was hearing none of this.

"Anna, I'm worried. What is this about? What is going on with you?"

"I just need some time to think, Logan."

"Anna, you've had a great deal of time to think. Look, if you are trying to let me down easy, don't. Just tell me. Don't string me along like this." There was an edge to his voice, but not anger. More like desperation mixed with frustration.

"I'm not stringing you, Logan. I'm trying to figure some things out."

"Either you love me or you don't, Anna. Either you want to be with me or you don't. Why is that so hard to determine? I know what I want. I want you. But not if you don't want me. I'm not that desperate, Anna. And I don't want to be your fool sitting around, pining after you while you're off on an island vacation with some other guy." Now there was a hint of anger.

"It's not an island vacation and he is not another guy." Marty could bear the pretense of ignoring my responses no longer and began to chuckle softly.

"Are you or are you not on an island? With a guy. A guy who is not me."

"Yes, but it's not a vacation."

"Oh? It's a business trip then?"

"No."

"Not business and not pleasure. OK, I give up. What is it? A retreat?"

"You're getting closer, actually."

"Am I?"

"Actually, it's a mission."

"A mission?"

"Yes, I'm helping my friend on a mission."

"What kind of a mission?" The bus rattled to a stop and the driver opened the door.

"Listen, I'm just getting off the bus now. Let me call you in a little while. Give me a couple of hours. Then I'll explain everything. Meantime, you can Google Missionaries of Joy."

The place where the bus stopped was staggering in its austerity. I would say it was blighted, but that sounds ugly. It was not ugly. It was old and dirty and broken. But not in a way that sunk my heart. I have been to ghettos before — driven through them — and each one took a piece of me, stole something from me. Maybe I was robbed of the idea that life is beautiful. The hope that it is. But Kingston was different. Maybe because I glanced over at Marty as we walked, and he was smiling. He looked in the eyes of the people sitting on deteriorating mats, rags hanging off them, looking like the beggars and the blind and the lame in Jesus' time. He looked in their eyes, as if he knew them, and smiled as if he recognized them from another place. One old woman reached up with her gnarled hand, and Marty took it in his and kissed it. A wide smile overtook her face, and she returned the kiss on his hand. I was waiting for one of them to say something, but neither did.

"It's just up here," Marty told me as we continued to walk.

Of course, we couldn't have gone the one and a half remaining blocks, without encountering another poor soul. There was a man, who looked more like a skeleton with skin, lying on the ground lengthwise against a decaying building. Fits of spasms rattled his body. The stench around him was horrible. It was clear he had been lying there for quite some time in his feces and urine. Flies swarmed him, and I spotted several other insects, of a variety I've never seen before, crawling over him, apparently without his knowledge. Marty stooped and put his hand on the man's shoulder.

"I will get you some help, brother," he told him. "I'll be back. Just hold on." The man closed his eyes.

At first sight, the mission house reminded me of the houses some of my friends lived in when I was growing up. They were small, one-story, three bedroom homes with carports, not garages, and no master bathrooms — just one shared bathroom in the middle of the house. The hallways were always narrow and the ceilings low, which made them seem darker than my more affluent friend's homes (and mine). I never minded this kind of darkness because it seemed there was the same amount of fun to be had in any size home. There always seemed to be just as many toys and games, just as many snacks in the cupboard and something entertaining in the backyard. My friend Rita lived in a three-bedroom home with eight siblings, so that was, of course, my favorite place to play. There was always something interesting brewing over there, given that the first five kids were boys. Blanket forts and sword fights and mixtures of kitchen ingredients that bubble up and might even explode (well, we thought so). One of those brothers showed me how to make a "magic rainbow" with a bowl full of milk, dish soap and food coloring. Each drop of color sits separately on top the milk, until touched lightly with a cotton swab dipped in soap. I won't say what happens because it's something that must be experienced firsthand, and I don't want to spoil it for anyone. After I saw it, at the age of ten, I wanted to learn everything I possibly could about viscosity and the internal friction of all liquid matter and the great, vast, open expanse of scientific discovery.

The mission house was sort of the direct opposite of great vastness. It was small and defined. Comforting. The first person we saw was a woman in her mid-20s, skinny with braids. Marty made the introductions, and she told us Father Julian was out and would return in about forty-five minutes.

"Is there someone who can help with an elderly man?" Marty asked. "He's only a couple blocks away."

"Brother Dylan is here. He could probably help you. Do you want to take the wheelchair?"

"Probably a gurney. This gentlemen is close to death. If he hasn't died already."

As the man lay on the fresh sheets of the gurney, he reached up with his boney hand, crusted around the knuckles and fingernails with something that looked like tar. He gazed vacantly into my face. I was afraid he would touch my cheek. His fingers came very close. He opened his mouth as if he was going to say something, but nothing came out.

"Here," Marty said, coming between me and the sick man and grabbing his outstretched hand. "Let's get you into a nice, soft bed and get you something to eat and drink. You will feel better in no time." Marty squeezed the man's hand. "I'll bet it's been a while since you've had a good home-cooked meal, huh, brother? That's one of the things they do best where we're going. They can cook, let me tell you. Oh mon. They can cook."

℠❖℞❖℠❖℞❖℠❖℞❖℠❖℞

My phone showed twelve unanswered calls that first evening. While I was holding it in my hand, it rang again.

"Anna, I thought you were going to call me. I've been worried."

"I'm sorry, Logan. There was so much going on. I got swept up in all of it."

"All of what, Annabel? What are you doing?"

"I'm just volunteering for a couple of weeks for the Missionaries of Joy. I'm helping out with impoverished, sick and disabled people."

"So, just on a lark, you follow this guy to Jamaica?"

"I didn't follow him."

"OK. Accompany him. On a mission."

"He has nothing to do with it."

"So you would have gone on this mission all by

100

yourself?"

"OK, maybe I am here because of him. But not *for* him. Not for romantic reasons."

"Annabel, just come home."

"I need to finish this out, Logan. It's only for a couple of weeks. Then, we can go out for a nice dinner."

I have to admit, the thought of sitting in a clean, quiet restaurant, eating a bowl of pasta with basil and tomato sounded really good. I so wanted butter bread. And a glass of wine would be nice. But not necessary. But bread, maybe even just plain bread. I hadn't taken time to eat all day.

"OK Annabel, I can see there's nothing I can do to convince you, so I will have to let you ride this one out. I hope you know how much I love you and miss you and how much I hope you will come back to me and say you want to spend the rest of your life with me."

"I know, Logan. You have been nothing but good to me. That does not go unnoticed."

"No, I have not always been good to you, Anna. And I regret every insensitive word I ever said to you. And I will live the rest of my life trying to make it up to you. I love you, Anna."

"Love you. I'll try to call tomorrow."

Not ten minutes later, one of the brothers came to tell me someone was on the phone for me.

"Bel, how are you? What are you up to?"

"Brad. How did you know I was here?"

"I called your cell and left messages, but you haven't returned my call."

"I haven't had my cell with me. How did you know I was here?"

"Logan told me."

"You called Logan? How could you do that?"

"I was really worried, Bel. You just dropped out of sight. My next call was going to be to the police. Why didn't you tell anybody where you were going?"

"I did. I told my family."

"What are you doing there?"

"All sorts of amazing things."

"Logan said you were on a mission."

"I'm just helping some folks out."

"When are you coming home?"

"End of the week?"

"Who's this guy you went with?"

"He's a friend of mine."

"Well, I'm obviously, and unfortunately, not your fiancé, but if I were, I'd be on the next flight to Kingston."

"Aw, that's very sweet and supportive of you to want to come join me in helping out."

"Actually, I'd take you — kicking and screaming if necessary — to the Ritz and order up a couple of Jamaican Kisses for us to sip by the seaside. But that's just me."

"Yes, Brad, that's you."

"You make it sound like there's something wrong with being me. I rather like being me."

"It must be nice to actually be your own favorite person."

"Oh, come on, Bel. All I'm saying is you work hard. You deserve a real vacation. You don't need to feel like you have to spend your time off working. You already do so much to improve the human condition."

"Except, I have never had an experience like this before, Brad. I couldn't have found on any resort beach what I have found here."

"Oh, Bel, you're forgetting all the great times we had on beaches. You didn't find any meaning in all of that?"

"Meaning? I don't know. What meaning did you find?"

"I find the answer to every question I ever had when I look into your eyes, Bel."

"Listen, Brad, I need to go help with lunch. I'll call you when I get back."

"Bel, I still need your answer."

"I know. I'm contemplating all of it, Brad. I intend to

give you an answer when I get home. I'm sorry it's taking me so long. If you need to find someone right away, I'll understand."

"No, Bel. I want you. I'll wait for you."

Finlay, a man with wild hair and a smile that occupies the majority of his face, charged me as soon as I got off the phone. "Mi wah ring di lunch bell. Can I ring di bell?"

"It's all right by me, but maybe you should ask someone who is in charge."

"Am I your favorite?"

"Yes. You are my favorite. Shhhh. Don't tell the others."

"Duh yuh think yuh could marry mi sometime?"

"Well, I would be honored, but I have to go home to Boston in a couple of weeks."

"So, let's get married tomorrow."

"I wish I could. But I have two guys at home waiting for me to marry them."

"You're a guh marry two of dem?"

"No, just one."

"But di odda one will be sad."

"Maybe for a little while. But he'll get over it."

"He can find someone else to marry."

"Right."

"But they won't be ers pretty as yuh."

"They might be prettier."

"Deh is nuh one ers pretty ers yuh."

"Well, even if that were true, beauty is not what makes a good wife."

"No, ah ow much a lady smiles at yuh. That's wah makes a gud wife."

Marty had come in through the kitchen and was smiling at the exchange. He winked at me from his post, transferring water in red plastic cups from a tire-sized tray to the long, skinny table that seated eighteen on each side. "You know? There's an old saying we have around here." Marty told me. "A big dawg's mout holds many bones, but a beenie dawg can be carried enna purse."

"What does that mean?"

"Well, beenie means small."

"OK." I stared and thought. "I still don't get it."

"Me neither. But if I could find fifteen minutes, I'd make a song out of it."

"Bob Marley, watch out."

"Are you a Bob Marley fan?"

"Not really, no." I pushed an elderly man in a wheelchair to the table.

"What kind of music do you like?" Marty asked me.

"Hmmm." I unfurled a napkin and placed it on the man's lap. He didn't seem to notice. "I used to listen to a lot of alternative. My Dad really loves folk music of the '70s, so I listened to a lot of that as a kid. I don't know now. I've kind of forgotten about music." Brad and I never went to a concert in the four years we were together, or even talked about music. And I'm not even sure what kind of music Logan listens to, if any.

"Can't imagine that. I've always got some kind of music playing," Marty said, momentarily holding an air guitar. "Either in my ears or in my house or in my car. In my own mouth."

"I have noticed you hum a lot."

"Used to drive my mom crazy. My girlfriend too. I think I have come to learn that women just like quiet. At least from me."

Later, on the front porch, I asked him, "What kind of music does your girlfriend like?" I asked him this, not because I was interested in the musical tastes of some person I've never met, but because I was wondering if I would get an answer like this:

"Oh, I don't have a girlfriend anymore."

"Have you ever come close to marrying anyone?"

"Yeah. I loved her very much. And she loved me. But I screwed up. She married someone else."

"I'm sorry."

"My Dad was an alcoholic and lied to my mom

constantly. So I grew up thinking that's just what you do. You lie. I had no idea normal people don't do that. Truth never meant anything to me. I didn't see it as anything worth going to the trouble for. Then, one day, my girlfriend left me. For lying, of course. I got drunk, I mean really drunk. I was not an alcoholic like my Dad, but I would sometimes drink and get drunk. So this time, I got so drunk, I nearly passed out. And I still don't know. Maybe I did pass out. But, anyway, it was like I was falling into this enormous pit. Dark, dark pit. Like no darkness you have ever seen before. You know, not like a room where all the lights are turned out. But complete, utter blackness. Pitch blackness. I can't even describe to you what it was like because there is nothing on earth so dark and no place on earth where you are so alone. And I was falling and falling. I had those pains in my stomach like you get when you fall, but I was falling faster than gravity normally pulls you, so the pain was horrible. It was like there was some force with double gravity pulling me down towards itself. And I heard a voice, *Deeper, deeper. The truth cannot find him here.* And then another voice: *Rejoice! The Truth has lost His son. He belongs to me now.* When I awoke, it was like my falling screeched to a sudden halt and I was in my bed, and I had this horrible stomachache. Not the usual nausea, but pain like I've never had before. And I understood that the pain was going to be eternal, that I was going to be falling forever into that bottomless pit unless I somehow changed. And I also understood that the lies were only the symptom of the actual problem. That I lied because I did not know Truth. You know truth with a capital T. I had that stomachache for six more weeks. Doctors could not diagnose it. But, obviously, I did not want to drink during that time, so by the time the six weeks was up, I was in the habit of not drinking, and I never got drunk again. The lying was not such an easy habit to break. But every time I lied, my stomachache would return, and it was not one of those stomachaches you can ignore. So, from all of this, I figured out that someone up there must really want me to stop lying. Someone up there must really care about me or else why would He remind me with this excruciating pain every time I was in danger of falling into the pit?"

"Do you still get them?"

"The stomachaches? No. I haven't told a lie in seven years."

"So that explains the straw," I said.

"Yes, I'm not taking any chances."

We were referring to the straw obtained from a very confused acne-faced kid the day we got our passports for the Jamaica trip.

We had just picked up a late lunch at Sam Burger's drive-thru and I asked Marty to make a stop at MacGuire's for some coffee since I had a headache coming on.

"I'm sorry," I said. "I know we just stopped, but if I'm going to have fast-food coffee, it has to be MacGuire's."

"That's OK. I understand coffee snobbery. Besides, it will give me a chance to get a straw. They didn't put any in the bag back there."

The MacGuire's drive-thru had five cars waiting when we got there, so we decided to go inside, where the line was shorter. While paying for my coffee, Marty asked the cashier if he could have a straw.

"Sure, they're right over there," said the teen, dressed in a red cap and yellow suspenders. He pointed to a batch of a hundred paper-wrapped straws standing in a stainless steel cylinder.

"It's not for the coffee," Marty told the kid. "It's for a drink I bought at a different restaurant. I'd be happy to pay for it."

"No," the kid said, almost annoyed. "You're fine. Just take it. On the house."

There are certain things you come to know about a person quite quickly in a place like Kingston. Things that could take much longer in the trendy restaurants or luxurious theaters of Boston. Seems that uncomfortable places lend themselves to talking about uncomfortable things. These are the things I came to know about Marty.

"I know the straw thing seems extreme," Marty says, hoisting himself onto the porch rail, "but I'm trying to make up for some of the harm I did."

"Does it work that way?"

"Maybe in some mysterious way. It's all I got to offer. It's worth a shot. And if it fails, I deserve whatever I get anyway. I played so many mind games in my younger years."

"What do you mean by mind games?"

"My girlfriend once planned a surprise trip to the lake for me for my birthday. She told me she was taking me out to lunch, but she just kept driving and driving until we reached this little lodge. When we got there, all my friends were there to celebrate my birthday. We went boating and had a picnic on the lake. It was so much fun and so thoughtful of her. And then, about a week later, she caught me in a lie. And I threw all that thoughtfulness back in her face. I reminded her that she too had lied to me about going to the lake. I wanted to prove that all people lie to each other. That it's just a part of life."

"I suppose everyone lies at one time or another. But hopefully no harm comes from it."

"I think there are very few lies that are harmless. Outside of planning a surprise for someone."

My dad used to talk about Lily's lies. It was a skill that came later than it does for most kids, but Lily made up for lost time by practicing often. She seemed to follow an unwritten flow chart. If something went wrong, blame it on Terry. If Terry denied it, blame Jimmy. If Jimmy denied it, stand your ground and repeat the accusation. If Jimmy produced an alibi, blame the cat. That's typically where the flow chart ended. Sunset rarely claimed innocence. And Sunset never had an alibi since she was pretty much a loner. Lily was really her only friend — at least the only friend allowed to pet her.

Lily got her just desserts when she married Frank. He

had a scapegoat too, but his was even more solid since his had a lifespan as long as his own. I once witnessed how this worked for him on a visit to their guest house.

"Who ate all the chocolate Cheerios?" Lily asked, into the open door of the food cupboard. "I wanted those."

"Ummm. Quacky Duck," said Frank nonchalantly.

"Quacky Duck does all the stuff I don- like." She closed the cupboard, scowled, placed a hand on her hip and pointed a finger at her husband. "You can- trick me, Frank."

Quacky Duck, Frank's rubber ducky friend since childhood, was responsible for a multitude of mischief in Frank's life, starting from the age of nine, when he showed up in Frank's Easter Basket. If I were to list all of Quacky Duck's transgressions, it would make a book the size of Webster's dictionary. So, I will just name a few. Quacky Duck never flushed the toilet. He often left the milk out. He many times neglected to clean up his crumbs. He left his smelly socks in the middle of the floor. He turned up the TV too loud. He left wet washcloths wadded up in a ball to invite mildew. He once spent Frank's entire paycheck on Lego Star Wars and then dipped into his savings to buy the $358 Death Star, even though he never built any of the sets the way they were intended and happily resorted to making his own random creations that, in the end, looked nothing like anything remotely close to the things in George Lucas' imagination. Quacky Duck also frequently moved other people's stuff and forgot where he put it. He drew silly faces on important receipts and mortgage bills. He had gas a lot. He snored at such high volumes that it kept Lily awake. He walked too close to the person ahead of Frank and accidentally stepped on the heel of their shoe. He turned the tuning knobs on Frank's friend's guitar when no one was looking. He once ate two packages of frozen hot dogs in one sitting. He fed the fish way too often and in quantities too large for the filter to handle. He tied various and unrelated objects together with shoe laces. For instance, he once tied Lily's favorite spoon (the one with the Winnie the Pooh on it) to the TV remote, in knots too numerous and too tight for Lily to untie, causing her cereal to become soggy as it sat waiting. Soggy cereal, soggy anything, was an absolute horror to Lily and to Frank. They both gave Quacky Duck a good talking to about that one. And ended up collapsed in laughter on the couch together.

The thing is, you never knew with those two how much was for drama and how much their perception of reality was really off. Were they pretending or did they really see the world that way? For example, one of the biggest puzzles to everyone except Lily was her sugar cookie recipe. She used the same one passed down by Beverly Greeley, who got it from her grandmother, who got it from her mother, and it probably went even farther back, but that's as far as its lineage had been officially verified. For generations, the recipe yielded plump, porous cookies, ideal for soaking up morning coffee. But something happened when it fell into Lily's hands. She was no slouch at cooking and baking, so her proficiency was not to be questioned. But success with that particular recipe eluded Lily every time. She never, however, seemed to notice. The horse-shaped cookie cutter yielded a blob that looked like a deformed pig. The rabbit-shaped cookie cutter produced a deformed pig with ear muffs. The cow-shaped cookie cutter resulted in a deformed pig with horns. The elephant cookie cutter yielded a deformed pig yawning. Frank and Lily were always able to tell what was what and even laid claim to their own favorites — Frank the horse and Lily, not surprisingly, the elephant. Lily had a fascination for wild animals that typically revealed itself in her vast volumes of pencil sketches.

Frank appreciated every one of Lily's pieces, especially the ones she would sign for him: "To Frank. My ♥." Spelling was never Lily's strength, so it took her until their wedding day to get his name right. She wrote it over and over again, at least thirty times a day, until she committed it to memory. Frank had no idea how hard she practiced, but he would have been impressed. He knew what hard work was all about. He had acquired many of his own skills the hard way, including cutting his meat and buttering his bread. It never occurred to him, until Lily, that butter does not have to be refrigerated if it is used up fast enough, which was never a problem in any home where Lily lived. So after they got married, Frank never again struggled with bread buttering.

Despite his clumsiness with knives and many other tools and utensils, Frank was good at a lot of things. In fact, there were a few things that just came naturally. A few surprising things.

Frank's older brother was a boy scout and taught Frank all he knew about ropes. From a very early age, Frank had a gift. Even the children who had no disabilities would ask him to tie their shoes, and Frank gladly obliged.

Frank learned quite a bit from his older brother, who held the title of best friend until Lily came along. Marco taught Frank how to speak Latin, for instance. The Stillwell Latin consisted of nothing more than putting "um" or "us" at the end of every word. "Passum the ketchupus." "I likus that shirtum." "Turn offum the lightus. Pleasum." So when one day Lily and Frank went to church and it turned out to be a Latin High Mass, Frank leaned over and whispered to Lily, "They singus this wrongus." This elicited in Lily such agonizing desire to laugh that she had to leave her pew, walk outside and rid herself of all thoughts of Latin. This worked. Until she returned to her seat next to Frank. Not that he dared say another word. But like an invisible thread, their thoughts passed between them and she knew he was thinking something funny. So she had to leave and return four times before the offertory.

It was one of those rare occasions when Quacky Duck could not be blamed, so there was no opportunity for deception. It was clearly Frank's fault.

Marty and I continued our front-porch discussion about the importance of honesty. "So, what happens one day when your wife asks you if she is fat?" I asked.

"I will answer with the truth."

"That she is fat?"

"No, that it is her love and goodness that makes her beautiful, not her ability to fit into a size 8 dress. I pray I will have the grace to never, ever lie to the woman I love again. That's how I lost the love of my life."

"You still love her, don't you?"

"With all my heart, I still regret it. And yes, I do still love her. I know that's probably wrong. She has a couple of kids, and I would never think of her in that way again — as a lover. But I know what I lost. I know *exactly* what I lost."

"As someone who has been lied to by the man she loves, I can tell you that I fully understand why she didn't marry you."

"Me too. Too late."

"Too late to be with her. But not too late."

"You mean I can start over. With someone else."

"Sure."

"I don't know. It hasn't happened yet in seven years."

"What would it take to make it happen again?"

"I don't know. Probably some kind of parting from my past. Some kind of assurance that I won't lie again to the person I love. You might wonder how I could, with such strong incentive not to. But when a skill is acquired as a child, practiced and perfected, it stays with you. And this was much more than a skill. It was a way of life. My mother was so busy dealing with the fallout from my Dad's lies, she didn't have time to pay attention to mine. So there was never a consequence to lying. Never a reason not to."

"So if people don't have a reason to tell the truth, they will default to the lie."

"Some people, yeah."

"Hmmm. That's interesting. I always thought truth was the default position."

"That's what normal people think. But for a certain number of poor, unfortunate meatheads like me..."

"What was your dad like?"

"I don't know. He hardly ever talked to me. He was always either too wasted or too busy thinking about how to stay wasted."

"Is he still alive?"

"Yes. He's in a home. Believe it or not, he outlived my mother, who never touched a drop in her life."

"How did she die?"

"Stroke. She always had high blood pressure. The stress of living with my father killed her. I'm sure of it."

"I'm sorry."

"She was a good woman. A saintly woman. The things she put up with. From my dad and from me. I wish I could do it all over again. I would take care of her, stand up for her, cry with her. She was too good to deserve any of our crap."

I looked into his face for a few seconds as he looked out on a row of dilapidated shotgun houses. Then, he looked into my eyes, and I looked at the houses.

"Do you have anything you regret so much it turns your stomach inside out?" he asked.

I tried to think and could come up with nothing. I knew there must be something. How could a 27-year-old woman have no regrets? Either she has been living in a hole in Bag End all her life or she is a shallow thinker. I honestly was not sure which one. I never thought of myself as shallow. But it is possible that Logan was right. I had had it too easy all my life. No difficulty or strife. Yes, I'd worked hard for my many achievements. But I'd been given the equipment to accomplish them. Some people are given the challenge without the equipment, and they are forced to invent. I had never invented or even reconstructed. I guess if I had to come up with a regret, it would be the time I wasted in angst over Brad. It occurs to me now that I do not know why he was dishonest. I don't think he is a habitual liar. I think he lied because he fell in love with someone else. That's something that could happen to anyone, I suppose. We were, after all, not married. Not even engaged. I doubt he is the type to cheat on his wife. And yet, I still don't trust him. I can't get past the fact that he kissed me one day and kissed her the next and then kissed me again the following day. I don't think that's officially considered cheating if there is no commitment on the part of any party, but it is not a pleasant thought. If he could hide something from me for that many weeks, he is too good at it. I don't want an accomplished deceiver.

Logan, on the other hand, is straight as an arrow. I can't imagine him lying. If he did, it would be to save someone's feelings. Most likely after he, himself, hurt them. He is often clumsy, but rarely malicious.

A man rode by on his bike and threw his hand up at Marty.

"Hey brother," Marty yelled. "Good to see you."

"Hey bredda, ow are yuh, Marty?"

"Can't complain."

"You bedda nah wit dat pretty gyal by yuh side. Ow long yuh be here?"

"Couple of weeks."

"I'll ketch up wid yuh."

We watched the man pedal out of sight.

"That's Keandre. He helps out here sometimes," Marty explained.

"A gentle soul."

Marty laughed. "You'd never know he killed someone when he was 15."

"What? Wow."

"Father Julian visited him in jail. And when he got out, he came to work here."

We both stared down the street, into the direction Keandre took, as if we might be able to discern something from the trail he might have left.

"Did you hear the reading at Mass today?" Marty asked.

"Which one?"

"The one about pouring new wine into old wine skins. I can't stop thinking about it. It seems like it is supposed to mean something to me, but I don't know what."

"Old wine skins."

"What does it mean to you?"

"I haven't a clue," I said.

A man who looked to be in his early thirties and walked a bit stiff-legged and slightly elevated onto his toes joined Marty and me on the porch.

Marty smiled and stood and placed his hand on the man's shoulder, looking at him as he spoke to me. "Annabel, I want to introduce you to a good friend of mine. This is Bennie. A man of few words, but a very mighty force."

Bennie glanced at me and then turned his head back to the side, trying to avoid any contact, even that which only loosely links a person to another person for a split second by the meeting of eyes.

I wondered if he feels anything like I did when I used to imagine, when I was a kid, that I had been in some sort of a catastrophic accident or suffered some sort of psychological trauma, and that I could not respond to anyone who visited me in the home where I was institutionalized. I could understand them, but I could not talk or respond in any way that would make them know I understood. I don't know why I wanted to pretend that. It is an odd sort of fantasy. Maybe because there is a part of me that has always felt a little disconnected. Which is maybe why I can entertain the idea of marrying Logan. His presence will not demand anything of me.

ജഃൃ

11

Popes with Marsupials

Miami International gives me that empty deserted feeling. I decide to make a call to John. I'm not sure what I will say or what he will be able to do to alleviate my desperation, but I call anyway. Although I have seen people cry at airports, I don't want to have any kind of emotional breakdown here, so I will say as little as possible on the phone. I hope he is as intuitive as he usually is. I want him to read my mind. I want him to hear it in my voice without me saying it: my heart is crushed.

He is on his game, and only thirty seconds into the call he asks me what's wrong.

"I went to Jamaica to find answers, John. But I'm afraid this trip eliminated any hope I had of finding them. Indeed, that there are even any answers to be found."

"Maybe you weren't so much looking for answers. Maybe you were running away from them."

"Where do you find yours?"

"I think you know the answer to that question."

"I think I do too."

"See? You already found one answer."

I wish I had some physical injury I could tell John about, some visible and painful sign that I had done something. But I had just stood there, dumbfounded. Or scared. I keep trying to remember. Was I stunned into immobility? Or was I fearful for my own safety? Why did I do nothing? Whose life was worth more? His or that of the Rhodes Scholar who can rid the world of human imperfection? Why, oh why, oh why did my feet not move?

Admittedly, I was already in a high mode of self-preservation. Kingston, Jamaica, is one of the most violent places in the world, and I kept worrying about Mom and Dad when they got the news their only daughter had been murdered. I felt guilty just thinking about the grief they would feel. I was there unnecessarily. I had no business there. I called them from the airport one day and told them I was on my way to Jamaica, with a guy I had just met, to volunteer to help the poor and disabled.

"Kingston?" Dad said. "Do you know how dangerous that place is? I just read a story. The U.S. State Department just issued a travel advisory. The protests are turning violent, the gangs are out of hand. Honey, you don't want to get on that plane. Believe me."

"Dad, we'll be careful. I promise."

"Is Logan with you?"

"No. I'm going with a friend of mine."

"I didn't think Logan would be crazy enough to do something like this."

"Look, Dad, we'll have lunch when I get back. What are you doing three weeks from Saturday?"

"So you won't stay out of Jamaica as a personal favor to me?"

"Oh, Daddy. I can't. Everything is all set. They're expecting me."

"How about as a personal favor to your mother? She's going to flip out."

"Daddy, it's not like I've never travelled, for Pete's sake. I spent four years abroad for college."

"Kingston is not Oxford, Annabel. You're soon going to find that out."

"I once got lost in Brixton and lived to tell about it."

"Well, if there's nothing I can do to talk you out of this, just please, please promise me you'll be careful. Will you let us hear from you every day?"

"Sure, I'll give you a call."

"Every day?"

"I'll try Daddy."

My father has always been over protective. I can't tell you how many times I complained about this to my mother when I was growing up. She would tell me that's just how dads are with their daughters, most particularly their only daughters. But one day, on my twenty-fifth birthday, she revealed the real reason.

When my mother was pregnant with me, and they told her I had Down syndrome, she was devastated. My father, having been raised with Lily, was not. He knew there would be struggles, but he also knew his wife was up to it. She was a strong woman, and smart. Devoted and mild in the day-to-day service of her family, but fierce as a wild animal when it came to protecting her young. She nearly took a coach's head off once for calling my brother a dingbat.

So my father was shocked when he found out his wife, who had always seemed like she could handle whatever life threw at her, was considering doing what nine out of ten people end up doing. She wanted an abortion. Well, she didn't *want* an abortion. She just didn't want an unhealthy child if there was a way around it. And there is.

Out loud, my father vowed to support her no matter what her decision. In silence, he prayed. He had never before prayed for much in his life. He was his Auntie Bev's son, and as such, never gave much thought to any kind of higher power once he reached his adult years. But for a good chunk of the time I was in utero, he did. He prayed his wife would choose to carry their child, whom he knew would be just like his sister, in all her charms and all her exasperating foibles. And this did not scare him one bit. He actually missed his childhood friend and quite liked the adult she grew into. But he never said a word to my mother. Never tried to influence her decision. It was, after all, her body, not his, and he had always believed the woman should have the choice. Plus, she would be the one to shoulder the lion's share of the work and responsibility since she was at home with the kids. A dread grew inside him each time he and Georgia saw the ultrasound, and the doctor would discuss their options. He saw his daughter moving inside his wife's womb and prayed the woman he fell in love with and married — the one who had grown into such a beautiful mother to his children — would not choose to destroy the life growing within her. He saw the ultrasound clearly and knew full well the contents of his wife's womb. And yet, he remained silent as she made the appointment for termination. The two of them exchanged few words about the decision, and my father began to view my mother as a heartless woman who would kill her own baby. Still, he said nothing except for, "it is your choice, Georgia. I will accept whatever decision you make." He would later learn that his wife was looking for direction from her husband, that she felt alone in shouldering the responsibility for the decision, that she was looking for any kind of sign from him that he wanted the child, but found none.

The day before the scheduled abortion, a letter came. It was from Beverly Greeley, and it was all about life with Lily. My mother cancelled the appointment the following morning, saying she may call to reschedule. Of course, she never did. But my father would be haunted by his own silence for the rest of his days. After I was born, the realization of what he had failed to do came crashing in on him as he held me for the first time. How could he fail to protect something so precious? At that moment he vowed to do everything within his power, and even some things outside of it, to protect all of his children. And that's why it appeared that my father spent his every waking moment, and probably his sleeping ones too, devising ways to assure that no harm would ever befall me. And aside from a skinned knee or two and a twisted ankle, the man succeeded. I was never allowed on a step ladder, and to this day, I am scared to death of heights. And I still cannot enjoy riding a bike for fear of all the things my father warned me might happen. I have always found the most comfort in quiet, non-risky activities, like reading and studying. My father, bless his heart, never had to deal with the realities of my dating because no boy ever paid me any attention. I made sure never to establish eye contact with a boy because I knew dating would be out of the question. I didn't even get asked to the prom. My father said that was fortunate since so many kids drink and drive on prom night. "Most dangerous night of the year." He said that about many nights throughout the year, depending on which one was coming up — Memorial Day, New Year's, Fourth of July. I think he even said it once about Ground Hog Day,

I was shocked, when I went off to college, and men all of a sudden noticed me. I took my hair out of its perpetual ponytail and got asked out on three dates within the span of a week. Guys at Oxford find smart girls attractive. It was interesting being attractive after all those years of being invisible. I wouldn't say it was more fun because I never relaxed enough to have fun. I always had the underlying, nagging feeling that something bad was going to happen and I always felt like a bullet dodger when nothing ever did. That feeling sky divers must have when they reach the ground and want to kiss it. I wonder why I never got that feeling when I left for Jamaica. Something about Marty made me feel as though nothing bad could ever happen.

For the first eight days of our trip, despite the crime and blight and poverty and disease, I still believed nothing ever could.

All day long, as I helped wrap people's sores and spoon porridge into their mouths, launder sheets and sing songs about Jesus with them, I looked forward to evening when Marty and I were alone. Not that I disliked the work, but I liked Marty more. We would sit together on the front porch sharing alternating stretches of long conversation and satisfied silence.

On the second Monday I was there, I awoke at 11:30, hot and feverish and feeling like I had to throw up. I rolled over on my side, hoping that would appease my stomach, but it made it worse. I sat up and looked at my roommates, sound asleep, worn ragged from a full day of service. My head began to swim and I lay back down and watched the ceiling spin. I knew in a matter of minutes, or less, I would have to run to a toilet, but I was afraid to stand up. If I fainted, who would find me? I felt, for the first time, too far from home, and I wished I could get on a flight right now, except the thought of the air sickness sunk me into a deeper nausea. I wobbled to my feet and made my way across the hall. I thought of knocking on the men's door, but that would wake them all. I cracked the door open a hair and peeked in, hoping I would not find anyone getting undressed or lying in bed in his underwear with his sheet on the ground. That is usually how my father slept, all the time I was growing up. Still not sure if he realized it. He would have his arms over his eyes and his pillow wrapped around his head, blocking out light and sound and any embarrassment that might have accompanied a realization that someone else was present to his boxer shorts and dingy well-worn T-shirt.

The crack in the door to the men's "dorm" revealed all were sleeping and no one had on boxers. Well, none had on *just* boxers. I stooped over, as if there was some kind of motion detector security system up high in the room, and slunk over to Marty, who was snoring slightly inside his long sleeping breaths. I stood over him, watching him sleep for a few minutes, summoning the nerve to wake him up. There's no way I could have done it, except I have never been so sick in my life.

Though I've never particularly enjoyed being sick, I almost felt fortunate to be in Marty' company and, at the times I was at my weakest, in his arms. Several times for the duration of that forty-eight-hour stomach bug, Marty had to carry me to the bathroom since I hadn't the strength to walk even across the room.

"The sickest I've ever been," he told me as he blotted my face with a cold, wet cloth, "was Christmas Day when I was seven years old. I was way too sick to get out of bed, so Santa snuck all my presents into my room. When I woke up, they were all lined up against my wall, on my bed. I always wondered how they got there without my waking up because I was not resting well. I had one of those half asleep half awake things going on like you do when you're really sick. I started to realize then that Santa was an even more amazing guy than I had originally thought. Later on in life I realized it was my mom who was an amazing guy."

"Oh, I had it pictured that your Dad was Santa."

"Oh no. My dad could not have snuck anything anywhere."

"Not the sneaky type?"

"Not the sober type. Sneaky, yes."

The first day back after being sick, I decided to take it a little easy. I thought about how my mother always told us to sit in the sun when we were recovering from an illness. I sat in the courtyard for just a few minutes before lunch. I shut my eyes and pointed my face into the warm sunlight. When I opened my eyes, the man who never spoke was standing over me. I noticed that his eyes were fixed on my watch. Its face was the face of a cat. Logan had given it to me for my birthday.

"You like my watch?"

He just stared. I put my wrist closer to him. He turned my arm over and examined the clasp as if to determine if he could open it.

"I'm Annabel," I said, taking his hand. "What's your name?"

He just stared at the watch.

"What's your name?" I asked again.

Still staring.

I pointed to myself. "Annabel." Then I pointed to him "Jim?"

No answer. Just staring.

"John?"

No answer.

"Frank?"

Nothing.

"Tom? Jerry?"

His gaze shifted from the watch to my face and a spark entered his eye for a split second. At least I thought I saw one. "Annabel," I said pointing to myself. I held his chin in my hand and looked into his eyes. "Who are you?"

"Mi," he said tentatively. "Mi." He rubbed his hand over his face from top to bottom repeatedly, starting from the hairline and ending at the jaw. "Bennie."

"Nice to meet you, Bennie." I felt a joyful exhilaration as I started to imagine and maybe even understand that this is why I was here — to reach through to some unreachable place. That's what one would have assumed. Anyone would have.

"I aredy met yuh before." He grabbed my arm and brought the watch closer to him, staring into the face of the cat.

"You like cats, don't you?"

"Mi lacka watches."

I unlatched the watch and gave it to him. He put the watch around his wrist and struggled to latch it with one hand.

"Mi lacka watches."

"Here, let me help you with that."

I latched it for him.

"Mi lacka watches." He smiled with large protruding teeth.

Brother Paul came from somewhere behind me and knelt down next to Bennie, placing both of his hands on Bennie's arms. "Praise God, Bennie, you are talking." He hugged the man, who noticed nothing but the watch. "I can't believe it, Bennie. You're talking."

"Bennie, can you tell what time it is?" I asked.

"Mi lacka cats."

News that the new girl had broken through to Bennie travelled quickly and soon reached Marty, who came to find me immediately. I had started to feel a bit weak and had decided to rest in the dorm with *Don Quixote.*

Marty leaned against the door jam, smiling at me. I don't

know how long he was there, but I noticed him when I got to the top of page 324. "Wow, Annabel, you got Bennie to talk. I'll bet that makes it all worth it — all that you've gone through to be here."

"Yeah. It does. Although, I don't feel like I've been through anything. I've enjoyed being here." I wanted to add "with you," but I didn't have the nerve.

"So, everybody wants to know how you did it."

"I have no idea. I didn't do anything."

"Just something about your presence, I guess."

"Well, I sure don't understand it. How is it that he, all of a sudden, opened his mouth and poured out complete sentences with near-perfect diction?"

"We see lots of miracles here."

"Miracles." I dog eared my page and closed the book.

"Yeah. This place is overrun with them. You want to hear a really big one?"

I stood up and joined him at the door. He was still leaning. "Sure," I said.

"I figured it was time for me to stop trying to pour new wine into old wine skins. So, I got me some new ones."

"New wine skins?"

"It had been over ten years since I went to confession. I decided it was time. I've had all this new wine coming into my life, but nothing to put it in except these old wine skins that kept tainting it."

"I'm sorry I'm not following you exactly."

"The graces. You can't hold on to them if you've got nothing to put them in. An old worn-out soul won't do. After Father Julian absolved me, I heard these words, as clear as if Father had said them. But he didn't. And I have no doubt who did. 'Behold, I make all things new.'"

"I wish I could believe what you believe. It is really so beautiful." I had been to Mass at the mission three times already. I love the smell of incense, the sound of voices reciting Latin in unison, the bells beckoning thoughts inward into something deeper, bigger, grander than what is outside. But how does one go about believing that God died on a cross? That God would have to be tortured and killed to save us? There are a multitude of other ways an almighty and merciful God would have chosen to save humanity, I am sure of it.

"It is beautiful," Marty agreed. "And it's true. That, of course, is what makes it beautiful."

"I wish I could believe, Marty."

"You're a scientist. You look to science for answers."

"Yes."

"But science doesn't offer any better answers than religion. Right before I came here, I went to a funeral for the newborn baby of a good friend of mine. She was a perfect baby, perfectly healthy, beautiful, easy pregnancy, no issues. Until the fortieth week when the umbilical cord got wrapped around her neck. Does that make any sense? You can't tell me science has an answer for that."

"And God does? What is God's answer to something like that?"

"The cross is the answer. The cross makes suffering mean something. Science just makes it random. I don't know about you, but I'd rather have it mean something."

"You know, sometimes you make more sense than all the geniuses I've been spending my time with."

"Where is the wise man? Where is the scholar? Where is the philosopher of this age? Has not God made foolish the wisdom of the world?"

"That's from the Bible, huh?"

"Corinthians. I've always been partial to Corinthians because I am one."

"You are from Corinth?"

"Yep. Corinth, Mississippi."

"Mississippi."

"Home to the Coca Cola Museum, Hog Wild Barbecue Contest and the annual Wildlife Tasting Supper."

I nod and smile.

"And the Northeast Mississippi Film Festival."

"Now *that* I could get into."

"Oh and Pickin' on the Square. I used to play at that."

"Sounds fun. I've been to Corinth. Greece. But I've never been to the south."

"You've been to Greece? What was it like?"

"Very beautiful."

"I'd like to go to Europe someday. But my life-long dream, ever since I was a kid, is to go to Australia."

"Really? Mine too."

"You've never been?"

"No, but I've wanted to go ever since my dad bought me a koala bear made of rabbit fur and the book, *The Koala who Came to Dinner*."

"I've wanted to go ever since I saw a photo of John Paul II holding a koala bear."

"I've seen that one. I love that picture. But I thought it was another pope."

"Benedict XVI?"

"Yeah, maybe."

"Maybe you are right. We can look it up." He grabbed his phone. I studied the deep lines in his forehead. "See? Here you go."

"Yup, you were right. John Paul II."

"Yeah, but maybe Benedict held a koala too. Let's see." He searches his phone again. "Yep, here's Benedict petting a koala bear. "

"OK, that looks like the one I probably saw."

"This was at World Youth Day in Australia."

"By the way, they aren't bears."

"Yes, sorry for that slip of the tongue. They are marsupials."

"How did we get on this topic, anyway?"

"I don't know. We started in Corinth and ended up in Australia."

I suddenly felt bad for correcting him, as if I am so much

smarter than he is and need to educate him. I should know how it feels since Logan does it to me all the time. Lily must have tired of such things. I remember Dad telling me that, for a two-year period in Lily's life, whenever anyone asked her what her favorite animal was, she would say "the sea lily." The person inquiring would then go on to clarify that they said favorite *animal*, not favorite *plant*. She would then go on to tell them that a sea lily actually is an animal, though it looks like a plant attached with a stalk to the bottom of the ocean. Lily liked to tell who ever would listen everything she knew, which was no small amount.

"The stems are their bodies," she would say. "The flower pedals are their arms. They scoop food into their mouths with all those arms. And if someone is chasing them, they run. They rip out of the ground. They use their arms to run and run and run. Like if a sea urchin is chasing them. Sea urchins are mean and hungry and they will eat them. They will take a bite out of their arms. So the sea lilies have to get away. So they lay down and use their arms to run across the ocean. Someday I gonna go scuba diving and see one. I saw a show once. The scuba divers got to see one run. It was really funny."

No one ever believed a word of any of this.

ಬ⋇ಇ⋇ಬ⋇ಇ⋇ಬ⋇ಇ⋇ಬ⋇ಇ⋇ಬ⋇ಇ

In Jamaica, the sun rises and the sun sets and the days just pass like that, one after another, and you don't worry about what the day is called. Monday, Thursday, whatever. After a number of sunsets, I knew a call to Logan was long-overdue. The longer I waited, the more nervous I was about calling. I summoned the courage and picked up the phone. He made it clear right away that he would wait for me as long as it may take, but he was losing hope as more time passed.

"There seems to be a recurring theme in my life lately. That I should marry the man who receives the lion's share of my smiles," I told him.

"It's not me, is it?"

"I don't know, Logan. I just don't know."

"Brad?"

"I don't know."

"The guy you are in Jamaica with then."

"I smile a lot here. But I can't tell you it is on account of Marty. It is on account of the goodness I find here, and for that, I owe Marty a great deal, including a few of my smiles."

"Do you owe him the rest of your life?"

I laughed. "He hasn't asked for the rest of my life."

"And if he did?"

"He hasn't asked."

"Would that give you cause for enough smiles?"

"Listen, Logan, it's getting late. I should go."

"Don't go yet, Anna. Let's talk about this. Tell me what will make you happy and I'll do it. I don't want to lose you. We've had too many important moments together."

His important moments. I couldn't think of even one of mine. When I'm with Logan, I feel like I'm on the outside looking in at this nice couple. They're well-matched and highly suitable for each other. Even-tempered and courteous. It's genuine enough for what it is, but what is it? Not passion, not romance. Not love in the magnetic sense of the word. Not deep friendship or even companionship. More of just togetherness. Which isn't bad, but what is the exact purpose of togetherness? Is it anything more than passing the time and sharing air molecules? And why is that an existence superior to aloneness?

Lily certainly believed matrimony was superior to the single life. After she got married, she wanted everyone else to get married too. Especially Pablo, her daddy. Every night, Lily would video-call him and ask him what he was eating.

"I'm having some scrambled eggs with some chopped up hot dogs, Mija. What are you having?"

"Grill- cheese. Frank like his with tomato. I like mine with cheese. And bread. Jus- bread and cheese. And I put on butter. On the outside. And cook it. Do you like grill- cheese?

"Oh yes."

"It Frank favorite. With tomato. Except for mustard sandwiches. That his number one favorite. I don' like mustard sandwiches. Blech. Mustard. I like mayonnai- sandwiches. That's good. I gonna have that tomorrow for lunch. What are you gonna have for lunch tomorrow?

"I don't know. I don't have much in my fridge right now. Maybe I'll go to the store. I might buy some chorizo. That would be better with eggs than hot dogs, huh?"

"No, hot dogs my favorite. And eggs my favorite. What's your favorite?"

"Well, I like all kinds of food. I don't know what my favorite food is. But I know who my favorite cook is. Her name starts with an 'L.'"

Lily grinned.

"And ends with a 'y.'"

"I know who that is." She grinned even wider.

"You guessed it? Yes, you are my very favorite flower, my sweet Lily. And now, I will let you go eat your dinner. Give my love to Frank."

"OK. I wish you will get marry, Daddy."

"Oh, no, Lily, I don't think there's any woman crazy enough to marry me."

"But if you get marry, you have someone to eat with."

"Well, maybe I will eat with my neighbor, Lenny."

"Is he nice?"

"Yes, and he's always hungry. So I know if I ask him, he will eat with me."

"OK. I love you, Daddy.

৪✿ఴ

128

12

The Third Prong

"What's Oxford like?" Marty wanted to know as he swung back and forth in the warm evening breeze, plucking the strings on his guitar, making up non-songs.

"It's amazing. I loved it. It's so old, so rich with so many stories to tell. And yet, so progressive in research and learning."

"Just the thought of it scares the heck out of me," he said, "You probably already guessed that I was never a very good student."

"No I wouldn't have guessed."

"I think you're smarter than that." He took his eyes off the neck of his guitar and smiled at me.

"Never cared very much about school?"

"Never cared very much about anything." He returned his gaze to the guitar neck and watched his own fingers move along the frets. "Except falling deeply in love. Often. Course most of those girls didn't even know I was alive."

"Pity for them."

He blushed and locked his eyes onto mine and continued to run his thumb lightly over the guitar strings. "I'll bet you were popular," he said. "Smart, pretty, kind."

"Bland."

"Bland? Far from that."

"I don't feel like I really belonged to life back then. I never really sucked it all in. It just kind of flowed by me. Like aquarium fish swimming past the stone mermaid."

"I know that feeling. Well, not of being a mermaid exactly. Maybe one of those cheesy toadstools, the red ones with the big white polka dots."

I chuckled.

"Or the replica of the Easter Island stonehead."

I chuckled even harder. "You know, you can fool some people, but not me. As you said, I'm too smart."

"What do you mean? How am I trying to fool you?"

"Not just me. You are trying to fool everyone. But I can see through it."

"What? If I was being dishonest, my stomach would let me know."

"No, you are not dishonest. Just deceptive. You are a closet intellectual."

He let out a hearty laugh. "Well, I think you are mistaken because I don't even know what that is."

"So you found school a bore and playing the A game a waste of time. That actually makes you smarter than the rest of us."

"Really? Then how come I get paid only a fraction of what those less smart people get?"

"Money isn't everything. You are not paid in dollars, are you?"

"No, more like cents."

"No, I mean, you find your reward outside your paycheck."

"I do. That is true."

"Tell me what that's like."

"What's it like?"

"Yes. What's it like being the bright spot in the day of so many people?"

"Well, what I do here is different, you know. Many of these people are desperate. But what I do at home, it's not about filling a desperate need. There is no void in the lives of the people I help care for. If anything, they are filling a void in me."

"Really? How so?"

"Hmmm. I don't know exactly. No one has ever asked me that before. You really do ask the tough questions."

"Yes, I have been asking a lot of those lately. I'm sorry."

"Well, to me, it's like I'm not fully alive unless I'm helping someone. Maybe that's some kind of psychological disorder. I don't know."

"Maybe. But I think it's beautiful."

ᔕ᙭ᘓ᙭ᔕ᙭ᘓ᙭ᔕ᙭ᘓ᙭ᔕ᙭ᘓ

I was feeding Mr. Ringo some porridge and decided I'd ask his advice. Not that he can answer. He was paralyzed and suffered severe brain damage when he fell off a three-story apartment building while fixing the roof.

"I don't know what to do, Mr. Ringo. I'm at this fork in the road, and I can't make a step in either direction. The stakes are too high if I do."

"You know, some forks have three prongs." A voice came from behind me, and I jumped, launching the porridge off the spoon. It splat on the floor halfway between the bowl and Mr. Ringo.

"I'm sorry," he said, swiping up the mess with his bare hand and wiping it on his jeans. "I didn't mean to startle you."

"What's down the third road, Marty? Or maybe I should ask 'who.'"

"Maybe someone you've yet to meet. Or no one at all."

"Hmmm. No one at all," I mused.

When Mr. Ringo finished eating, Marty and I took our favorite spots on the front porch.

There were quite a few minutes of silence while we rocked in our turquoise-colored metal rockers and watched lethargic people and unleashed dogs walk by.

"Can I ask you a question?" I said.

"Sure."

"Have you ever thought of you and me?"

"You and me? Together?"

"Yes. Together."

"To be perfectly honest, yes. I have thought about it. A lot, actually."

"Me too." I said.

"Really? Would it work?"

"I don't know."

"It's nice to think about."

"It is." I smiled at him. "What exactly do you think about? I mean, when you think about you and me?"

"I think about making up songs with your name in them. I think about long walks together in the woods. Waking up every morning and finding you there. Watching the sun rise, drinking coffee, reading the news, talking about our world. Sitting on a porch swing with my arm wrapped around you, your arms wrapped around our little one. Rocking you, rocking our little one. Washing the windows with you and squirting you with the garden hose. Cooking pasta together while listening to Mary Chapin Carpenter. Having a towel fight. House hunting for the perfect little fixer upper and laying tile together. Writing you love notes and hiding them in your briefcase. Greeting you at the door every night with a friendly kiss and on Friday nights with passionate kisses. Sitting in the audience at our grandchildren's Christmas pageant. Taking them to the county fair. I think about combing your silver hair for you, driving you up the mountain road to where we had our first date, parking and looking out at the Valley and thinking about all we've seen together and thanking you for all you have allowed me to feel, all you've allowed me to be. But mostly, I think about writing songs with your name in them."

"Wow. You've given this quite a bit of thought."

"I have. Far too much, I'm sure. What do you think about?"

"I think about you writing songs with my name in them."

Marty smiled.

"So have you?" I asked.

"Have I what?"

"Written any. Songs. With my name in them?"

"You put me on the spot."

"I'm sorry."

"No. Don't apologize. I do some of my best work when I'm on the spot. Don't go away."

He went inside and came back with his guitar. I can't remember the exact words of the song he sang to me, but I was amazed he could make it up out of thin air, if he indeed did. I could picture him up late in the middle of the night for three nights straight, strumming and jotting, pick between his lips, and scratching out and replacing the pencil behind his ear and strumming again and humming and then singing half-lines and shaking his head and singing full lines, scratching out and strumming again, singing with a satisfied smile. Well, that's what I pictured. But he wanted me to assume he had made it up off the cuff, so I didn't press to learn otherwise.

"Can I ask you a very bold question," I said, "one that is none of my business?"

"You can ask me anything."

"How many other songs have you written with a girl's name in it?"

"Just one."

"Don't worry. I'm not going to ask you to play it."

"Good." he smiled. "Do you want to hear one I wrote for my sister when I was 14?"

"Sure."

"She died when she was a baby. I was nine when she was born. There were four kids between me and her. She was born with all of her intestines on the outside of her body. Normally, that's something that can be corrected with surgery, but she had a heart condition on top of it and didn't survive the operation. I remember my mother, who never, ever, ever questioned anything, yelling up into the ceiling the night she died. 'Why?

Why? Why?' she was screaming. And I just remember thinking, 'silence.' There was just silence from whoever she was screaming at. No answer to her question. And there never would be. Even at nine years old, I knew that. There could never be a good answer."

"I'm so sorry."

"But then I grew up. And I realized I was wrong. There is an answer."

"Really?"

"Yeah, I don't know it. But I don't have to. God knows it."

"I guess my question for God would be why allow a baby to die? Well, not that question exactly, but why allow a person who is going to die after only a few days to live at all? What was the purpose of that short life?"

"I don't know. Maybe Jeanie changed us all in ways we don't even know she changed us. My mother was always a good mother and a good woman. But there was an edge to her. After Jeanie, she was different. That baby somehow took the edge off my mother. Maybe she started to understand what was really important in life. Maybe she appreciated her kids more. Maybe the small stuff just didn't seem important any more. I just know I was never yelled at again for forgetting to take my shoes off at the door or forgetting to flush. I got yelled at for plenty of important stuff, but not for leaving the lid off the toothpaste."

"How does it make sense that a person would have to die for that?"

"No, a person had to live. Jeanie had to come into being. Then she had to leave. That's what changed my mother."

"And if she had never been born? Or if your mother had given birth to a different combination of egg and sperm? A healthy combination that would yield you a sister whose companionship you and your family could still enjoy today. Wouldn't that have been better? How could it not be?"

"But that's not how it happened. It is what it is, and nothing can change that. We just trust it was how it was supposed to be."

"But the suffering."

"Part of life."

"But if you could avoid it, why wouldn't you? What's the purpose of unnecessary suffering?"

"What makes it unnecessary? Besides, I don't know that it is avoidable."

"Let's assume for a minute that it is avoidable. Shouldn't it be avoided? At all costs? At what cost should it be embraced? For what payoff is it worth it?"

"You might have to ask one of your smart boyfriends that question, Annabel. I don't know the answer to that one."

"I'm quite sure they wouldn't either."

He noodled on his guitar some more, looking up the neck at his fingers, though he didn't really need to look.

He began to sing.

Like a comet
You came and went
a flash across our hearts
a trail across our souls
You're still burning bright
And we're still growing old

Can't believe we won't see you again
Not until eternity
Can't believe we'll never hold you,
Until time sets us free

You must come around
every 4.5 billion years,
That's how long the world waited
And that's how many tears
we'll cry until we see you again
Yeah, that's how many tears we'll cry

For some reason, that song is in my head as I sit now at Miami International, waiting for my flight to Boston, which has been delayed twice, once by forty-five minutes and then again by an hour. I have forgotten the song with my name in it, but I remember Jeanie's. I've been trying to figure out why that is.

The woman sitting across from me is wearing a T-shirt with a graphic of someone who looks a lot like Betty Boop holding a wine glass and proclaiming, *Wine is the answer. What was the question?*

The older woman sitting next to her has a T-shirt with a wine glass on it and the description: *Grandma's sippy cup.*

I assume they have gone to Napa Valley together as a mother-daughter bonding trip. I miss my mom and contemplate going to see her in Minneapolis instead of going home to Boston. I'm not due back home for several more days. Logan and Brad don't even know yet I cut my Jamaica trip short.

I think about how endearing it is that the two women are both wearing their wine shirts. And then I think about Marty's wine skins. And the voice. *Behold, I make all things new.*

Oh, how I wish it were so right now.

I look at my wrist. The tan line is still there, in the shape of the cat watch.

I still don't understand what broke Bennie's silence.

"Bennie, how come you waited until now to speak?" I asked him one day.

"I ave been speaking since di beginning. Inside mi head."

"Why did you never speak with your lips before?"

"I neva loved anybody before. Yuh know, except mi madda."

"Where is your momma now?"

"I doan know. I hope shim ah nah dead."

"When did you last see her?"

"I doan know. She left mi. I doan know when. Shim ah poor an had nuh food. I hope shim ah nah dead."

"I'm sure she is fine."

"Ow duh yuh know?"

"Just a feeling."

He looked at the watch again and it was like something in his brain turned off again. I didn't want him to return indefinitely back into his silence. "So, Bennie."

He looked at me, blank, like the first time I saw him, and I was afraid he wouldn't talk again.

"You just chose not to speak until one day you wanted to speak?" I asked.

He shook his head and looked off into the distance. "I doan think I chose nah to speak. I just could nah speak until I wanted to speak."

I had to think about that for a minute.

"Love made mi talk," he clarified. "Mi love yuh, Annabel. And cats."

Over the next few days, whenever I saw Bennie, he would smile at me and point to the watch and give me a thumb's up.

And I would say, "Is the watch still working, Bennie?"

"Yah."

One day, as Marty and I were on our way out, I heard a shout.

"Hey!"

"Oh, hey, Bennie," I said.

"Weh yuh going?"

"To the market."

"Ow come?"

"To pick up some rice and some fruit."

"Can I come?"

I looked at Marty.

"I don't think we're allowed to take you with us, Bennie," Marty said. "Not on this trip. I'm sorry. But we'll bring you something."

"Anodda watch?"

"I don't think they have watches where we're headed, " Marty said, "but if I see one, I'll get one."

"Fah har," he said pointing to me. "Fah Annabel."

"For me?"

"Cah yuh gave mi dis one."

He stared at the cat watch for quite a while, seeming to forget we were there, slipping back into the place he'd been for the past twenty-some odd years.

"Bye, Bennie. See you in a little while."

His eyes didn't break from the watch. "Likkle more."

"Likkle more," Marty answered.

"Which means?" I asked.

"See you later."

"Likkle more, Bennie," I said.

The streets were crowded with small cars, bikes, buses and pedestrians. Coronation Market, sprawled out under well-weathered tents and canopies, exploded with color and slang and grit. Higglas, down for the weekend with their produce or shoes or electronics, tried to convince passersby of the quality, value and desirability of their goods, using words and phrases that I had no hope of understanding. It took me a while to accept the fact that Jamaican Patois wasn't just some kind of an accented English, but a language unto itself that I wasn't going to decipher overnight, if ever. It is a combination of British English and African, finding its origin in the necessity for slave owners to communicate with their African slaves.

I thought I heard my name within the noise. I glanced at Marty, but he was deep in conversation with a higgla, apparently talking about the gigantic green mango or whatever it was he was holding. I scanned the market in a 360-degree search and then focused back on some strange red fruit or vegetable (I couldn't tell) cut open, shaped like a heart embedded with three large black pits. Then, I heard it again, and this time it was unmistakable. How many Annabels could there be in any given crowd? Much less in Jamaica. I scanned the crowd and found Bennie across the road. He was waving, limp-wristed and expressionless, his eyes locked on me.

"Bennie, what are you doing here?" I hollered over the clamor of the marketplace.

"Getting yuh a watch."

"No, it's OK. I don't need a watch. I have a phone that tells time. We better get you back to the house. They will wonder where you are."

Now at this point my memory dissolves into blurred images that wash through my brain like waves of nausea. Bennie stepping into the street. Marty screaming from behind me.

I am frozen.

Marty's footsteps pounding heavy. The truck barreling closer. Marty colliding with Bennie. Orange steel. Yellow steel. Two bodies flying. A woman's scream. Was it mine? Can paralyzed people scream?

Then the half-second silence. Bloodied asphalt. Writhing, weeping. Then Yelling. A swarm of panic.

I am still frozen.

A life-saving flurry. Dialing. Ripping shirts. Tying. Pressing wounds.

I am still frozen.

Sirens. Sirens. Sirens.

The writhing stops.

I crouch down and sob. I have lost Marty. I just found him. And now I lost him.

My feet did not move from the place where I first heard Bennie call my name. I am smart enough to do the calculations. I was twenty feet closer to Bennie than Marty was. I will tell you, if my feet had moved, I could have beat the truck. I could have pushed Bennie out of the way and remained completely unscathed and we'd all three be safe now.

What kind of a human being freezes?

I look into my second cup of vending machine coffee. It is empty, and I consider getting more, but it would require traversing half the airport terminal. Plus, for some reason, I can't unlock my eyes from the black and grey tweed sweater worn by the man sitting opposite me. It reminds me of something. I can't figure out what.

I am not expected home for several more days. I rebooked my return flight from Jamaica after the accident, cutting the trip short. I wanted to get out of there. But the problem is, now I don't want to go home.

I've got to tell my parents where I am. My mother answers the phone.

"Honey, how are you doing? How's the mission?"

"I've left Jamaica."

"Why? Where are you now?"

"At the moment, I'm in Miami, waiting for my connecting flight." I don't understand why, but Lily's face flashes through my mind. Or through my soul, more precisely. What comes out of my mouth next surprises me. "But I'm not getting on that flight,"

"You're not? Why?"

"I'm going to Seattle."

"What? Back to Seattle? Why?"

"To get a snow globe for Miranda. And I need to see Beth."

"Is everything OK, Annabel? I'm worrying here."

"I just need to talk something over with Beth and John."

"You're not OK, Annabel. What's wrong?"

"Oh, Mom." I want to tell her, but the tears are pressing at the backs of my eyes, and I don't want to cry. Not here. "Don't tell me you're becoming a worrier too, just like Dad."

"Only when I need to."

"Listen, I just wanted to let you know where I am. I'll call you later, OK? When I get to Seattle."

"Honey, why don't you come to Minneapolis instead. We haven't seen you for so long."

"Maybe I'll stop back through on my way home from Seattle."

"We would love that, Honey. We'll go clothes shopping

and see some movies."

Sounds terrible to me, but I appreciate the love behind it. "Love you, Mom. Call you soon."

I watch a man set his guitar down to fish something out of his wallet. A wave of grief washes over me as I realize I will never hear Marty play again. Father Julian has his guitar now. He and the brothers will make good use of it. They sing all the time. Joyful songs. Ridiculously joyful songs.

I return my phone to my purse and it rings again.

"Annabel?"

"Hi Daddy."

"I was sitting here thinking, maybe I should ask you if you want me to come with you?"

"You were? To Seattle?"

"Yes. I could meet you there."

"You could?"

"Sure. Should I?"

"That's very nice of you, Daddy, but you have to work, don't you?"

"I can call them and see if they can get me a replacement."

"No, Daddy, it's OK. I just need some time to think and sort things out. I'll call you when I get there."

"So, you're OK?"

"Yes, I am. Please don't worry."

"I have to worry. That's my job."

"And you do it very well." For the first time in my life, I don't find his protectiveness annoying.

"Call me if you change your mind, OK, Jelly Belly?"

"OK." I feel a weak smile move onto my face.

"And I hope you find your answers," he says.

"Thank you, Daddy. I don't know if there are any. But thank you."

I hang up the phone and watch a man with a well-trimmed dark brown beard look up information on the kiosk. I remember when my dad used to wear a beard and it was dark like that. When it started coming in gray, he shaved it. I wish he would let it grow again.

And now I have another question to add to my list: Why is it, with all the men in my life, all I want right now is a hug from my father?

෨✳ଔ

13

The Things Lily Knew

The man in the tweed sweater sits in front of me. Since we are both sitting in aisle seats, I will see his left sleeve the entire flight, diagonally across the entire nation, from Miami to Seattle.

I contemplate the number of difficult words that lay ahead of me. I don't want to tell Logan what happened in Jamaica. I'm sure he'd put his arm around me and agree that it must have been a horrific experience to witness such a tragedy. Then he'd tell me to go get my coat so he could take me to see a movie and get a bite to eat. He's not going to understand why I'd rather sit on the couch and stare at the wall. For the next year. Or two. Or maybe longer. I know he will tell me I need to try to snap out if it, cheer up, move on.

I decide to call him now, in hopes that maybe telling him on the phone will allow us to skip all of that, so when we finally do see each other, I can get right to the wall-staring part. Only, for some reason, the circuit between my brain and my finger malfunctions and I dial Brad instead. It is shocking to hear Brad's voice and if I wasn't stunned into silence for a few seconds, I might have called him "Logan." The mere thought of doing that is horrible, though maybe it would serve him right considering what he did to me.

I start to feel guilty for thinking that way. And maybe that guilt makes me start believing I owe him something. Or maybe I just need someone to practice on. So, I tell him what happened in all of its entirety. Or most of it anyway. So Brad ends up being the first person I tell, and I decide at this moment that I don't ever want to tell anyone again.

"What happened was out of your control and not at all your fault," Brad says with his typical air of certainty. "You really need to move past this, Bel."

"In other words, just get over it."

"I don't mean to sound insensitive, but yes. Lamenting is going to do nothing to change the past. Move forward and pour your energy into making the world a better place."

"By joining your company?"

"I really think devoting your time to this project will do you a world of good, Bel. And it will do the world a world of good."

"I don't know, Brad."

"You know, if you and I weren't a thousand miles away right now, I would take you in my arms and kiss you. At length." My head swam back to a simpler time. Back to a time when a kiss from him meant something.

"I'm sorry, Bel. Now I've probably really confused you. I promise I will keep it strictly business if that's what you want."

"I don't know what I want, Brad."

"Yes you do. Tell me. I'll try to make it happen, Bel. Just tell me."

"I want to go back. I want to recapture what you and I had. But we can't do that, can we? It's already all changed."

"So, let's change it back again."

"I don't think that's possible, Brad."

"So there's no such thing as second chances?"

"Sounds harsh, doesn't it?"

"Doesn't sound like the Bel I know." He sighs. "Look, Bel, I would do anything for you, you know that. But I can't wait forever for your answer."

"Yes, yes, I know. You would do anything for me. Except wait."

"I didn't say that. I said I can't wait forever."

"Well, if you want my answer now, I will give it to you."

"But I won't like it, will I?"

"I don't think so."

"Then, don't give it to me."

"OK. How about I give it to you next weekend? I'm going to pay a visit to my cousin and then I'll be home."

"You're running away again? This will be, what? The fourth time? I don't think running has been very effective in helping you find the answer."

"I'm not running, I'm flying."

I don't want to tell him my real reason for wanting to return to Seattle. That now, more than ever, I need to know the things Lily knew. I want to find the place where she and Frank are, bring her flowers and him some sticks, and lay there in the grass between them until I somehow become un-stuck. I picture something like time-lapse photography, the sun sets on me lying there between their graves. The sun rises and I am still there. Clouds roll. The sun sets. The sun rises. Clouds roll. The sun sets. The stars twinkle. The sun rises. And then, the answer comes to me, and I kiss the ground where Lily lies.

"Don't over-think it, Bel," is Brad's advice as the turbulence rattles the plane and the man in the tweed sweater moves his arm off the armrest. "You've got a tendency to make things more difficult than they have to be. What does Logan say about your flying away again?"

"I haven't told him."

"Really?" I could tell his brain was doing the calculations. I had called him before Logan. "What's he going to say?"

"I don't know. Probably the same thing you said."

"Guys aren't very original, are they?"

"Not really, no."

"OK, look, Bel. I'm going to ask you a very direct question, and I would very much appreciate a direct answer. Are you in love with me, Bel?"

"Yes."

"Really?"

"Yes."

"Really!"

"Yes."

"Well, then, what's the big question? I'm in love with you. You're in love with me. I don't see how there's anything but one answer."

I stay quiet.

"Unless you are in love with more than one of us."

"I do love Logan. He was there for me when you weren't."

"But you can't marry someone out of gratitude, Bel. You marry the person who makes your heart skip a beat and the person you have the most in common with. We share so much together, Bel. You've got to admit. There couldn't be two better suited people in the whole world."

"Frank and Lily."

"Frank and Lily? Who are they?"

"I told you about Frank and Lily. I want what Frank and Lily had."

"Oh, your Aunt Lily. Well, I'm afraid to have what they had, we would both have to lose a significant number of IQ points. I'm not sure the trade-off would be worth it."

I'm not sure if I should be offended on behalf of Lily or if I should try to find truth in what Brad says. Maybe he has a point. Maybe sheer bliss is not within reach of the highly intelligent.

The man in the tweed sweater returns his arm to the armrest, and it hits me. I know now what that sweater reminds me of.

It had been Frank's lifelong dream to compete in the Iditarod, so Lily decided the next best thing was to get him his own sled dog, or at least one that is bred to pull sleds. For someone who works in an animal shelter, finding a dog, even a very particular kind of dog, was not so difficult. Lily waited for the perfect husky, and one day he came. Fish had been found wandering in traffic without tags. Wandering is not unusual for huskies, who are probably the most untrustworthy of all breeds off the leash. They are programmed to run. And stop to pee. And run some more. And pee. Not sure how that peeing thing works on the 1,000-mile Iditarod. Fish always took three or four pee breaks on his trek around a city block. Frank and Lily got a harness for him (extra large) and looped his leash to an old radio flyer wagon they found in Jake and Terry's garage.

For the three years they owned that husky, Lily and Frank looked like wookies. They wore that dog everywhere they went. A good number of dogs shed. That doesn't begin to describe what huskies do. Huskies blow their coats. You can pull tufts of hair off them, like picking cotton, and it doesn't make a dent. You can see the hair flying off them as they run through a stream of sunlight. I guess working under the same philosophy that when life gives you lemons, you should make lemonade, Lily decided when life gives you husky hair, you should make a sweater. It didn't take too many thrice-a-day brushings before Lily had harvested a tall kitchen garbage bag full of fur that she intended to make into a sweater for Frank. She thought it would look most epic if Frank and his sled dog matched when they made their trek around the neighborhood. She had planned to ask someone who makes sweaters how to go about turning fur into yarn, but she never knew who exactly to ask because no one she knew made sweaters. Frank passed away before she could even begin the project. Fish died four weeks later.

ဆံ✿ભ✿ဆံ✿ભ✿ဆံ✿ભ✿ဆံ✿ભ

Aunt Terry is happy that I want to stay in the guest house. I want to be where Lily was. I want to understand what her life meant. Not to other people. But to her. And Bennie's life. What did his life mean? He closed out the entire universe and lived inside himself alone. Right up until the time when he came out, to talk to me, and then something horrible happened. None of that makes any sense to me. What was the purpose of all that? What is the purpose of Bennie?

"Maybe he's a teacher," Aunt Terry offers as she exits the freeway. I remember this route from the airport to her house and not much has changed about it since I was a kid. It makes me feel as if all my days have melded into one. That there is no distinction between my childhood and my adult days, that I am still the same as I ever was, still a child and still a teen and still a young adult and whoever it is that I am right at the moment and maybe even, if I extrapolate, I am already an old woman, looking back over the entirety of my life, wondering where it all went, how it could have passed in such inexplicable haste, how the mysterious acceleration of time went, for the most part, unnoticed even by someone who is prone to motion sickness as I am.

"Maybe he teaches the rest of us compassion," Aunt Terry continues. "Gratitude."

But what does he mean to himself, I want to ask. I won't ask this out loud, but for his own sake, not the world's, would it be better had he not existed? If he had any good times throughout his life, were they enough to make the suffering worth it?

"Think of Lily," Aunt Terry says, adjusting her rear view mirror as we sit at a red light.

"She loved her life, huh? She had genuine joy."

"On a daily basis. Probably on a minute-by-minute basis. Frank too. Not uninformed, thoughtless, brainless bliss. That is not what they had. That's what they would have had if that was all they had. But they had more than that."

"What did they have?"

"They had the full spectrum of human experience, and therefore, they had joy and they had sorrow. Lily shed her share of tears, you can bet. Frank too. Particularly toward the end. His final year was so hard on everyone."

I remember John telling me one time that he found Frank sitting in the middle of the floor crying, his head cradled in Lily's arms as she rocked back and forth. This was just after his dementia had set in.

"What's the matter?" John asked, fearing that they had just gotten news that someone died.

"His dragon friend fell apart," Lily said solemnly. A pile of Legos lay beside them.

"Oh, well that's easy," said John crouching down. "We'll just put it back together."

"No, you can't," Frank wailed. "I don't remember how I built him. He had three heads. He has to have three heads to eat this kind of food." He picked up a fistful of yellow Lego bricks in an assortment of shapes and sizes.

"No, Frank, all dragons eat that kind of food," John assured him. "It doesn't matter how many heads they have."

"Yes it does, John. You don't know nothing about dragons. Just get outta here!"

"Shush, Frank," Lily said. "That's not nice."

"It's OK, Lily," John said. "Frank is just upset. Do you want me to try to help you rebuild it, Frank? We could make him even better."

He sniffled and shook his head, hanging it low. "I will never like him better. The only way I will like him is if he is the way he was. He was my favorite."

Lily understood Frank's pain. Earlier that year, they had gone to the beach and found a gigantic sand palace, built by a professional sand castle builder who had been hired for a seaside wedding. Next to the elaborate structure was a heart with the couple's name written in the sand: "Ivan loves Donna."

Lily decided to build a sand castle of her own, right next to that fancy one. She made Frank snap a picture of her with the two castles — one that looked like something out of Architectural Digest and the other that looked like someone had packed sand into a bucket and a Styrofoam coffee cup and then turned it over. That, indeed, is what someone had done.

Lily was equally proud of hers as I'm sure the Sand Man was of his. The sad thing is the next day when Frank and Lily went to go visit her creation, it had been stomped to the ground.

The Sand Man's castle still stood, and even Ivan and Dana's names had not weathered. But Lily's castle appeared to be deliberately kicked down by someone.

It's a good thing the castle had been built as far away from the ocean as it had because that volume of tears falling into the sea might have caused some kind of global event.

Who knows how long Lily's tears might have continued had Frank not had the brilliant idea of snapping Lily's picture in front of the Sand Man's creation and telling everyone she built it.

I stare out Aunt Terry's twelve-passenger van window at the Seattle shoreline and picture Lily there, smiling, eyes so squinted the lash-lines arc like rainbows. That gigantic sand castle looms behind her.

"Annabel, Honey, what happened in Jamaica?" Aunt Terry asks. "You seem to have a dark cloud hanging over you."

My phone rings. It is Logan. I have been ignoring his calls, but I decide to take this one. Probably to save me from Aunt Terry's question.

"Annabel, where are you? Are you still in Jamaica? The mission said you'd left. Why don't you answer your cell?"

"I took a little detour, Logan. I'm in Seattle."

"What? Again? Why Seattle again?"

"I need some answers."

"Answers? I thought you went to Jamaica to find the answers. You can't trot all over the entire universe looking for answers, Annabel. The answers are not out there. You have to find the answers within yourself."

"Well, I know that's what all the Disney princesses ultimately discover, Logan, but I have nothing within me at the moment. So that's why I'm searching the universe."

"Where are you staying? Why don't I fly out and meet you there?"

"No, Logan. It won't be long, and then I'll be home."

"Is your friend with you? What's his name? Marty? Is

Marty with you?"

"No."

"Please, Annabel, you have me worried. Very worried."

"Don't worry, Logan. I'll be fine."

"I just don't understand the running, Annabel. If you are looking for a way to tell me you don't want to marry me, if you're afraid to tell me—"

"No, Logan, it's not that. I just really don't have the answer. I wish I did. I know it's hard on you."

"What about Brad's offer? Have you come up with an answer for him yet?"

"No. I'm afraid I don't have any answers for anybody." Really, I could have just ended that sentence after "I'm afraid."

৪০⌘জ⌘৪০⌘জ⌘৪০⌘জ⌘৪০⌘জ⌘৪০⌘জ

Lily became a great artist because she was always drawing. She was attached to her pencil and paper in the same way many kids get attached to their camera or video recorder, seeing a photo or video op in every moment and every situation, from a close-up of a friend's salad to a neighbor scuffing out in his flannel robe to pick the newspaper up off his lawn, to an ant carrying a crumb across the sidewalk.

Lily would turn herself completely around in the bleachers at a game or in the pews at church and sketch family portraits of the people sitting behind her. No one ever seemed a bit uncomfortable about this. On the contrary, her subjects always had smiles on their faces. Sometimes she would tear the page out of her book and give it to the people she had drawn. Other times, she would bring it home and put it in her large collection of drawings stored in a plain corrugated cardboard box.

I feel myself smiling as I sit surrounded by boxes in the middle of Lily's living room floor, looking through her artwork. Terry has allowed me the privilege of bringing Frank and Lily's stuff in from the shed, sorting through it, organizing and labeling the contents of boxes, and making piles for charity of whatever belongings do not have sentimental value. Organizing is Aunt Terry's forte, but she hadn't wanted to tackle it right after Lily died, so everything was packed away in the shed, where it has stayed for close to a decade.

What to do with all these sticks? There are hundreds of them in various boxes and containers, but I wouldn't dare think of discarding one. I can see them through Frank's eyes, and they all do look different. I'll bet he knew them all individually. Lily probably did too, because they were important to Frank. I mark the boxes "Frank's sticks" and tape them up again.

Onto a box of photographs. I guess Lily was one of the few people who preferred paper to digital. There were so many pictures of her and Frank together. They were smiling in every one. She also had a huge number of photos of herself with Bev, taken in the nursing home. Bev was smiling in many of them as well, except at the very end of her life, when her muscles just couldn't manage it. Lily's smile remained big enough for the both of them.

Enfolded in a newspaper clipping were a number of snapshots of Lily, grinning from ear to ear, arm in arm with various important people. Lily with a state senator. Lily with the governor. Lily with a movie actor. Lily with a county attorney. Lily with a TV anchor. They were all taken on election night. It was the night Lily got to vote and became a news story because she had fought for that right in a court of law and won, just before scaling the steps to the bench and throwing her arms around the judge and planting a big kiss on his ample cheek.

Tucked in between two of the photos was a napkin with a number of autographs on it. One of them said, "Glad to have met a hero like you," and was signed *Governor Schmid.*

At lunch time, Beth brings fried chicken and we sit on the floor among Frank and Lily's boxes and eat right out of the bucket.

"I'm just not sure what my life is supposed to look like,"

I tell her, licking grease off my fingers.

"That's always a tough one," she said with a mouthful of chicken. "But I do know that even when you're living the life you're supposed to live, it never looks like it's supposed to. There is nothing I'd rather do than be a mom, right? But you'd never know it sometimes. I sat there at the dinner table one night, and I had this thought: how could I be annoyed at every person at this table — for something entirely different. Talk about multi-tasking. I was mad at one kid for not knowing how to eat a chicken wing, taking little ineffective nibbles, afraid to get barbecue sauce on her upper lip. I was mad at the second kid for sticking her entire hand in her mouth to suck off the barbecue sauce since I had just confiscated her napkin because she was dipping it in her water glass and sucking the liquid out of it. I was mad at the third kid for eating with her mouth open and taking heavy, annoying breaths between bouts of chewing. And I was mad at the fourth kid, my husband, for laying his whole upper body on the table as he clutched the wing in his elbow-propped grasp." And I was further mad at him for being oblivious to all my madness, happily harboring the basket of napkins at his end of the table, neglecting to take note of the fact that the two children nearest him were wearing more sauce than the chicken was. All of this annoyance, from four different sources, I was able to bear in one single place in my body — between my upper and lower molars, clenched together so tight, there was no hope of any food passing through them."

Beth tosses a chicken bone into a plastic bag and reaches for another piece. "And then Michael says to me, 'Aren't you gonna eat, Honey? These wings are really good.' I wondered, how did he know I was not eating? How did he happen to take notice of his surroundings? What strange disruption in the cosmos had occurred?"

I hear stuff like this and it makes me question my wisdom in trying to decide who to marry. The question is not who. The question is *why*. Why do people willingly, being of sound mind and body, sign up for such an existence?

Beth has to go pick up her kids, leaving me alone again with Frank and Lily's stuff. The heavy meal has made me sleepy. I lie down amid the boxes, which nearly entirely encircle me and cut off my view of everything in the room except for a painting hanging above the couch. It is a cluster of helium balloons tied to a bicycle parked in front of a sidewalk cafe in what could be France or Belgium. Sitting next to the bike is a bull terrier that looks like the puppy Pablo gave Lily. The dog is holding a stick. It reminds me of Beth's style, and I wonder if she painted it. My eyelids fall as I try to remember that dog's name. Pablo Puppy, I hear Lily say, and my eyelids fall.

When I awake it is dusk. My hip hurts from lying on the floor. I hobble to my feet and step around the boxes, moving closer to the painting, making out the signature in the bottom right-hand corner: "Beth Lovely."

Maybe Beth had given it to Frank and Lily as a wedding gift. I want to see if Beth wrote anything on the back. I take it off the wall and flip it over, finding nothing but blank canvas. On the wall where it had hung is a heart, about the size of a pie pan, drawn in ball point pen. Inside the heart are the initials F.S. + L.S. Whoever gave the room a fresh coat of paint did not have the heart to paint over Lily's love for Frank and Frank's love for Lily. The wall right around it was Tuscan gold, while the rest of the room had been repainted a Latte cream. I understood why. I would not have been able to paint over it either. And so there it is, and there it will stay for as long as there are house painters and room decorators who value love. And I wonder, what evidence would there be of the love between me and Logan ten years after our death. I can assure you we won't be writing on any walls.

ಬ⚹ಣ⚹ಬ⚹ಣ⚹ಬ⚹ಣ⚹ಬ⚹ಣ

I wish I could have seen John again, but he left for a vacation in Europe the day I flew in. Traveling seems to be good for his depression. Maybe I'll plan a trip out of the country soon.

Australia would have been next on my list if you had asked me several weeks ago. But not anymore. I can never go there now. Maybe Hawaii.

Aunt Terry and I sit out in the moonlight on lawn chairs, drinking coffee, strong and dark, the Seattle way. She is trying to answer my many questions about love. She has sensed that my "who" has turned into a "why."

"Let's say two people get married because they love each other," she says. "But it turns out that she nags and mettles in all his business, and he is boring and just doesn't understand her and doesn't want to take the time to try. They've both changed so much or gained so much knowledge of the other, that the two don't even resemble the man and woman who originally fell in love. So why did they get married?"

"Because they loved each other at the time. They didn't know how it was going to turn out."

"Right. And so now what do they do? Now that they know?"

"They put up with it for the rest of their lives?"

"Right. They do. That's where real love kicks in. They choose to stay. They make the choice to love."

"Uh-huh." I sip my coffee and nod, as if I understand.

"So life is really very simple. When things change, you love. When things stay the same, you love. When things turn out the way you planned, you love. When they turn out different, you love. When people do what's expected of them, you love. When they let you down, you love."

"That still doesn't tell me which man to choose to love."

"You are paralyzed right now because you are afraid of love. You are afraid of what it will require of you. You are trying to make the choice that will bring you only happiness at no cost. And there is no such choice. Love always costs something. If there is a choice without cost, it is probably not love."

But, I want to say, I already made the choice against love. I made a choice not to put myself between the speeding truck and Bennie. It cost me nothing, and I lost everything. Aunt Terry moves her chair close to mine, puts her arms around me and lets me sob into her soft camel-colored sweater. I am well aware that cashmere is dry-clean only and I don't want to do any more damage to it. I grab a napkin from inside my sweatshirt pocket. Aunt Terry reaches inside her jean pocket and pulls out a tissue. She blows her nose, and I look into her face and realize her eyes are moist. She is remembering something. I want to ask her what it is.

"Annabel, Honey, I have never told this to anyone who comes to see me." She wipes her eyes and blows her nose again. "But I think it's time for you to go home now."

I want to apologize for overstaying my welcome, but I know Aunt Terry and I know that's not what she means, and I don't want to make her feel bad.

"Honey," she grabs my hand and squeezes it. "You can travel the whole world looking for answers, but that's not where you're going to find them — in the world. There is an answer to every question, and it's the same answer. It's what I have told every one of my children and foster children since I learned it myself. The answer to every question is love. What is love calling you to do?"

"You mean whose arms do I want to run into right now?"

"No. I mean what does love require you to do at this moment?"

"Love requires I do the impossible."

"No. Love never requires that. Love doesn't make those kinds of demands. If love is demanding it, it is possible. Most likely not easy, but possible."

14

New Wine

I have been sitting in my car staring at his door for twenty minutes now. He has a green door with three small windows across the top. I wonder what it looks like from inside the house when the sun streams through the windows onto the floor. I imagine a small area of tile right by the door and then carpet throughout. I picture beige. I would rehearse what I will say to him, but I am at a complete loss for words. I should probably go home and wait until the words come. My keys are still in the ignition. I turn the key halfway and the dashboard lights and air conditioning turn on.

No, I cannot be so cowardly. I turn the ignition key back again.

I open the car door and walk up the short path, across the freshly-manicured lawn. I see someone peek out the window. It is not him. Two men come to the door, one short and short-legged with a thick neck, the other knobby and long-boned. They both have open mouths.

"Hi," I said. "Is Marty here?"

"Yes," the one says. Both remain motionless.

"Can I see him?"

A voice comes from inside the house. "Who is it Dennis? Is someone here?"

"A lady," the skinny one says.

"A pretty lady," says the short one.

"Is she selling something?"

"Are you selling something?" the skinny one asks.

"No," I smile. "I just came to say— hello— I guess."

"Oh, hello." The short one smiles big at me with his missing teeth.

"Hello," I say. "Do you think I could say hello to Marty too?"

"Marty, the pretty lady wants to say hello to you." Both sets of eyes never leave me.

"OK. Coming." His voice strains a bit, as if he is getting himself up off a couch. Then, he appears in the doorway behind the skinny and short man. He looks momentarily confused and then a smile grows wide across his face. I am relieved he is glad to see me.

If I am going to be honest, I will tell you that all the time in Jamaica, up to the moment when Bennie wandered into traffic, I thought maybe Marty was the one — the "none of the above," the one who makes me smile, the alternate and unlikely choice everyone was telling me might exist. But after the accident, I couldn't bring myself to even face him. I didn't know if I ever wanted to see him again. It's not his injury that has kept me away, or at least I hope it's not. It's the profound and all-consuming guilt that consumes me when I even so much as think of him.

"Annabel," Marty's voice catches a little on the "bel." "Well, come on in. Please." He steps between the two men and pulls gently on my arm, until I am across the threshold, and then he takes my hand. "How are you?"

"I am fine, Marty. How are you?"

The two men still don't take their eyes off me. They have turned around, leaving the door gaping open.

"Oh, these are my friends, Dennis and Jimmy," Marty says, closing the door.

"Hi." I lift my hand slightly.

"They've been here helping me out with unpacking and laundry and cooking. I don't know what I'd do without them."

"We're helping him learn to do everything with one

arm."

"Come on in and sit down, Annabel," Marty says motioning to a taupe micro-suede couch. I was right about the beige carpet. Pretty much everything in the place is some shade of brown or grey. It is one of the most unimaginative decors I've ever seen. And Marty, of course, is not a dull person. I figure he must put all his creativity into his music. I suddenly remember again. He won't be playing any more.

"I'm so sorry, Marty." I think about taking his hand, but I feel strange since he has only the one, and I know if I hug him, I will dissolve into tears. So, I sit on the boring couch. Dennis and Jimmy have followed after us, standing and looking.

"Would you like something to drink, Annabel? Or eat? Are you hungry?"

"No. No thank you, Marty."

We both smile at each other for a few seconds. Something buzzes. It's coming from the hallway. Dennis and Jimmy look at each other. "Clothes are dry," Jimmy says. "Let's go get them." He speaks very precisely, pronouncing every letter, like a computerized voice.

"So. Annabel." Marty smiles.

"Marty, I am very sorry for leaving you in Jamaica. I should have come home with you instead of leaving early, without you. It was a cowardly thing to do, to just run away."

"It's OK. My friends from the group home have been taking good care of me — helping me make sandwiches, cleaning out the fridge. It's good for them too."

"How are you adjusting?"

"It's a little difficult. But I am just so glad I'm alive. I've never been hit by a truck before, but I never would have guessed I would live through something like that."

"I am so sorry, Marty. It's all my fault, and I am very sorry."

"Your fault? How is it your fault?"

"I had time to make it to Bennie, but I just froze. I am so sorry."

"No, no. That's not true. None of this is your fault."

"Yes, it is. I've done a great deal of thinking about it. Lamenting, actually. I have replayed it over and over in my brain, and I know this to be fact. I could have saved Bennie and none of us would have gotten hurt."

"We have no idea what would have happened if you had run into the street. You could have tripped and been killed. Bennie might have been killed too. But we are all still alive. We have to thank God for that."

"But your arm, Marty. How will you —"

Marty got down on his knees before me and grabbed my hand. "I want you to look at me, Annabel, and really hear me. Given the chance to change anything, I wouldn't. I would gladly do the exact same thing over again. I don't regret anything, Annabel. And I don't want you to, either."

"I'm just sorry I didn't stay with you in the hospital. Why did I leave you?"

"No looking back, Annabel. No looking back. If God has forgiven you, you have to forgive yourself. You are not larger or wiser than God. Are you?"

"How do you know God has forgiven me?"

"I just know."

I don't know why, but I look into his gentle eyes, and I believe him.

"My cousin Beth took me to the airport when I left Seattle," I tell him. "She gave me something to read on the airplane. Kind of a memoir. She's never let anyone else read it. She has kept it hidden in the bottom of a drawer since the day she finished it. She told me she considers her life began again on the last page. It was as if she was made totally new. I wanted to be new again. So I made a silent vow to myself when I took the journal from her hands, I would read it through to the end and do whatever she had done to make herself new.

I can honestly tell you I never could have guessed what I was promising myself. I know Beth pretty well and I didn't think she could have possibly done anything as horrible as what I had done. But when I read what she wrote, I understood I was wrong. So, I figured, if she could be made new somehow, so could I. And that's when I found myself calling Father Julian. I asked him if he could hear my confession on the phone."

"You what?"

"Yeah, I did. I called him from the restroom on the airplane and asked him to hear my confession right there on the phone."

"Um. Did he?"

"No. It was a really stupid thing to ask. But I was desperate."

"I can take you to my parish. You can make an appointment with Father Lucci."

"No need. Father Julian happens to have a number of friends in a mission house here in Boston and called them up and made an appointment for me to see one of them as soon as I got off the plane. I drove straight to the mission from the airport."

He smiles wide. "So you have new wine skins."

I nod and smile back. "And new wine. And I think that's probably the only reason I can be standing in your presence right now. Well, sitting. I didn't think I was ever going to be able to face you again, Marty."

"That, for me, would have been a bigger tragedy than losing an arm."

"Really?" I want to cry. He thinks that much of me.

"Really."

"Listen, I better be going. I've got a big day ahead of me tomorrow." We both stand, and he walks me to the door. We can still hear Dennis and Jimmy folding clothes in the kitchen.

As I pause at the door, he gently takes me by the arm and gives me a kiss on the forehead. "I pray that you find all the answers you are looking for, Annabel."

಄⚶಄⚶಄⚶಄⚶಄⚶಄⚶಄

The post office has two full crates of mail for me. I dread

the hours it is going to take me to sort through it. I resolve to wake up an hour early every morning and open mail until it is finished. This is what I find on the first day:

"Dear Annabel,

Here is the video I told you about when you were asking about those photos of Lily. This was filmed during a fund raiser/tribute to Lily. People were very generous. We were able to raise $20,000 for the animal shelter. Cue it up to your dad's speech at 32:16. It is precious." Lots of Love, Aunt Terry

"There are things Lily said that people simply didn't believe," Dad says as he stands out in front of the shelter, putting his hair back down on the top of his head each time the wind picked it up. "They thought she was delusional. Lily was not delusional. She was very much in touch with reality. But when she told people certain things, they made certain assumptions. They didn't assume she lied, necessarily, but that she made things up. When she referred to her husband, for instance, they thought it was cute. They assumed she had a good friend whom she believed she was married to. When she told them she had once been the Homecoming Queen at Hooper High School, they didn't believe that either. Maybe it's hard to believe that a group of young people could be so good as to think up such an act of kindness and go about implementing it, campaigning for Lily, printing up *Lily for Homecoming Queen* buttons and convincing the majority of the student body to cast their vote for her, beating out the smartest girl, the most beautiful girl, the best-dressed girl and the most athletic girl on campus. I can hardly believe it myself, but I was there, and I witnessed it with my own eyes. I witnessed the way the homecoming king, Josh McInnis, strapping good looking guy, took her hand and kissed it and then grinned ear to ear when Lily grabbed his face and returned the kiss on his cheek with a mighty force that might have been downright painful for a guy with a less formidable bone structure. People also didn't believe her when she told them she had seventy-two dogs. But she indeed did. She treated every dog in the shelter as if it was her own. She thought of them that way. She knew most of their names and the few she couldn't remember she just called "Roscoe." Nobody knew why. But that was Lily."

The phone rings. I press pause on the DVD. It's Brad. I would give Logan the courtesy of being the first one I spend time with after the trip, but Brad tells me he's at the curb.

"Aw, Brad. I'm still in my pajamas."

"That's OK, Bel. You always look pretty."

"I haven't even had my first cup of coffee."

"I'll make it for you. Or we can go get some breakfast. Come on."

"OK, give me a second to change."

He is more handsome than I remember when I open the door and find him leaning against the door jam, dressed in a tight-fitting blue and green plaid shirt, tailored khaki pants and brown loafers. His pose is quintessential Brad, cocky and yet somehow endearing.

He puts his hands on my upper arms and kisses me on the cheek. "It's so good to see you, Bel." He breezes past me into the family room and sits on the couch. "It seems like you've been gone a year."

"Seems like that to me too."

"How's your friend doing?"

"Marty?" I sit on the couch, leaving a cushion-sized space between us.

"Yeah, Marty."

"He's adjusting. Thanks for asking. And you? How is your work."

"Fantastic. I can't wait for you to join me."

"I did a lot of thinking about that, Brad."

"I know. It's been quite a long stretch of thinking."

"The thing is, I'm not sure you and I see things quite the same way."

"What do you mean?"

"I want to tell you a fable I heard in Jamaica." I sit on the opposite end of the couch.

"OK." He slides over next to me, puts his arm around me and leans in close. "I'm all ears."

I try to tell the story without sounding nervous. I am afraid my voice will shake. I have to concentrate on keeping it steady.

There once were two birds. One was black and one was a brilliant yellow. The yellow bird sat on a high branch, singing a beautiful song. Everyone liked to gaze upon the yellow bird, and when they did, it would warm their faces and they would dance and sing. They also liked to look upon the black bird because it knew many tricks and would delight and excite people with its swift maneuvers and captivating patterns it drew in the sky. But just when the people least expected it, the black bird would flutter its wings and a stream of ashen dust would fall into the people's eyes and they would cry. The people came to resent the black bird and they sometimes even threw rocks at it. They failed to understand that their tears were necessary to water the desires of their hearts and that without it, nothing would grow inside them. One day, the two birds found love inside each others' hearts and they joined their hearts together. When they did, a third bird appeared, this one with feathers of every color, brighter and far more beautiful than the yellow bird and exceedingly more agile and entertaining than the black bird. And when the people saw this, they knew their folly in resenting the black bird. Without it, the rainbow bird could have never come to be.

"Very insightful," Brad says with raised eyebrows.

"Yes. The person who told this to me was a very old man. He calls himself Crazy Eddie. That's what everyone has always called him. He hears voices. Most of them are just annoying, like the ones who tell him to shake the curtains or slap the wall with the spatula. But occasionally he hears the voice of a narrator."

"He made that story up?"

"Well, the narrator in his head did."

"Pretty good story for a crazy guy. Or a crazy guy's narrator even."

"Yeah. That's what I thought too."

"So, the moral of the story?"

"Where would we be without the rain?"

"No rain, no flowers?"

"No rain, no rainbow, more specifically."

"Or even more specific — no rain, no rainbow bird."

He brushed the straggles of hair off my forehead. "I know this is off topic," he says, "but right now, I feel like giving you a very long kiss."

"That is off topic."

"I'm not going to, I just thought you might like to know that's what I want to do."

"Thanks for letting me know."

He kisses my hand. "Thanks for sharing Crazy Eddie's story. Now, about the job."

"Well, I was getting around to that. I was asking Crazy Eddie what he thought, and he seemed to think it wasn't the right fit for me."

"You're looking for career guidance from an old guy who suffers from insanity? What kind of sense does that make?"

"Crazy Eddie is perfectly sensible. He is crazy, but he is also wise."

"I'm beginning to wonder if what Crazy Eddie has is contagious. Now *you're* talking crazy."

"I know I am. I wish his wisdom were contagious. Unfortunately, I do feel a little crazy. I still don't know what answer to give you."

"I don't know why, I am not surprised. Anyway, just out of curiosity, what did Crazy Eddie advise you to do? About the job."

"He didn't give me any advice. He just told me the story about the birds."

He closed his eye and rubbed his forehead. "OK, tell you what. I hate to put this decision off any longer. But why don't you sleep on it one more day. Sound good? I'll call you tomorrow. We'll have lunch."

"We'll have to make it Friday. I'm tied up for the next few days."

"Bel, this really is crazy. I can't wait much longer for your answer. Time is of the essence and I need to find someone who can partner with me as soon as possible."

"I think you better find a back-up plan."

"I won't need one."

"You're that confident, are you?"

"I'd say there's a 99.9 percent chance that you and I will be partners." He stands up and adjusts his waistband. "We're going to be like Crazy Eddie's bird and spread our rainbows across ten thousand tomorrows."

৪০৯৫০৪৯৫০৪৯৫০৪৯৫০৪৯৫০৪

My old mail is still piled high on my kitchen desk, and the carrier brings still more. There are two letters in the mailbox when I walk out to check it after Brad pulls away. I open the first one, addressed in pink ink, with large rounded letters.

Dear Annabel,

Thank you for cuming all the way here jist to give me a nuw snow globe. It was very, very, very, very, EKSTREEMLY nic of you. Wen my furst one brok, I thot God was tring to punish me for bing selfish and fiting with my sister. But mom ekspland it was sum thing that hapend becuz of sum thing I did, not becuz God did it to me. But I am sooooo happy to hav a new won now! I hav never told anybody this befor, but wen sum thing bad hapens, I ask Lily for help. I dont reely no her, but I seen picshers and my mom toks about her all the time, so I no she is woching over me. I tok to her all the time, and sum times she ansers. She is kind of like an imajinary frend, like my frend

Gina has, but Lily is reel. I askd Lily to ask God to send me anuther snow globe and He did! I love you, Annabel. I hop you will come and vizit agin soon.

Love, Miranda

This is the second letter I open:

Dear Annabel,

I pray you are well and that your friend Marty is continuing to heal. Beth told me of the job offer you received, and I wanted to share some insight with you, for what it might be worth to you. I hope you don't mind my unsolicited opinions, but you feel like one of my own, and you know how "mothers" are...

I don't exactly think mine is the right attitude to have because we are not meant to hinge our happiness on one person, and I know this is a strange thing to say, but it's how I feel. So here goes: I don't know if I could have been happy without Lily. I know I live without her now and I'm not unhappy, but that is because she lives somewhere in me still. But I feel like I couldn't have been happy without having known her.

Do not misunderstand what I am saying about happiness.

I am not saying there was no cost to loving Lily. As I told you when you were here, love never comes without a cost. Only suffering and sacrifice earns you the right to call it love. And let me tell you, the people who lived with Lily earned it.

There were all kinds of costs. Emotional, physical, financial. Sometimes costs that took every last bit of what you had to offer. But mostly, it was day-to-day small exasperations, and some not-so-small ones.

Like the time Lily messed with the thermostat just before everyone left for a three-day trip to the mountains and heated the house to 89 degrees for an extended weekend.

Then there was the time she forgot to secure the hamster cage door with the necessary twisty-tie, and Timbledee Sniff got loose. He was found in the master bedroom closet, with a stash of cat food, which he had apparently stuffed into his elastic cheeks and carried down the hall from the laundry room.

Coincidentally, right after that, the all-in-one printer stopped working. I went out and bought a new one and put the old one in the garage. Months later, when I was clearing things out to give to charity, I decided to nicely wind the cord, so it could be more easily transported. That's when I noticed the small chunk missing from the rubber coating. On closer inspection, I could see that the copper wire within the rubber casing had been partially severed. I put my magnifying glasses on for an up-close inspection and discovered that the cord was covered in what looked like tiny tooth marks. I took the printer inside and plugged it in using another printer cable, and what do you know? It powered up with its friendly series of clicks and an optimistic "ready" display on the screen. Which means I spent $289 on a new printer when the old one was perfectly fine. It just needed a new $7 printer cable — one that hadn't been chewed by a hamster. Pulling out the computer armoire to confirm what I already knew, I saw the old familiar signs of Lily's very small playmate — droppings and paper shreds courtesy of Mr. Sniff. I felt rather silly for not checking the printer cable in the first place, and from then on, whenever a printer went bad, it was the first thing I did, though that never proved to be the trouble at any time in the future. Murphy's Law reigns.

Beth wanted me to tell you that Jolene passed away. I guess she had told you a little bit about her. I regret that I didn't get to see her before she died. I don't regret it for my sake, but for hers. I don't think hers could have been a good death because I don't think she could have had much peace. But maybe now everything will be clear to her. It will be a painful clarity, but a clarity nonetheless. Please pray for her soul.

It was great to see you out this way, Annabel. Hope you can make it again soon. (And next time, I won't tell you to go home.)

Praying for you to find all the right answers and peace in your decisions.

Love you!

Aunt Terry

I go back inside and lay the letters in the opened pile, next to the huge stack that still needs attention. I'll get to those later. Right now, I have a phone call to make.

"Hello, Brad."

"Bel! My beautiful Bel. What's up?"

"I've made a decision, Brad. I don't want to keep you waiting for it any longer because my mind is made up. I really appreciate your offer, but I'm not going to take the job. I'm going to marry Logan."

"I had a feeling," he says and then there is dead silence and I was trying to figure out how to fill it. "But that doesn't mean we can't still work together, Bel."

"It just wouldn't work. I decided it's one or the other in my life. You or him. Not both of you. I can't marry one of you and work with the other."

"Then, marry and work with the same one."

"Are you asking me to marry you?"

"Yes."

"Why?"

"That's a silly question. You're in my blood, Bel I never got over you. I never will. And you yourself admitted that you still love me."

"I'm sorry, Brad. I just don't trust— Can't trust that you—"

"Bel, I am sorry for what I did to you. And I wish I could go back and undo it. But all I can do is throw myself at your feet and beg you to believe I learned my lesson and will never do anything like that again. Can't you release me from my past, Bel? Why does the past have to define our future?"

"And where is Shana right now?"

"Where is she?"

"Shouldn't you be making these promises to her? She's your girlfriend du jour. Aren't you doing the same thing to her that you did to me?"

"That's different, Bel. I've never been madly in love with Shana. She's a nice girl, but she is not right for me."

"And when will the day come when I am not right for you?"

"That day will never come."

"That day already came and went. You don't remember?"

"So, let's start over. Let's count this as Day One."

"Doesn't work that way, Brad. I'm marrying Logan. I'm sorry."

"Well, my heart is broken. We would have made a great team. We could still be business partners, though. I wish you would consider it. I promise to keep it strictly business."

"Well, all these questions of romantic interests aside, I have to admit to you that I am not all that crazy about the project."

"Not crazy about it? Why?"

"I've told you about my Aunt Lily?"

"I don't know. Probably."

"My Aunt Lily had Down syndrome, and I can tell you, and I'm learning more and more every day, that there are many things about our family that just wouldn't be the same without Lily.

"So, Down syndrome is a good thing?"

I have to think about this for a second. "I'm not sure what my life would have been had Lily never been. I don't know that I would have been the person I am without her. I don't know that I would have been here at all. But I can say these things for sure: being smart is not the key to happiness, if happiness is indeed the purpose of life. See, that's something I don't even know. But I bet she did. I bet Lily knew the purpose of life. No, Brad, I can't say the world would have been a better place without Lily."

"OK," Brad says. "But would you have not given Lily a pill, if you could, to improve her intelligence? To reduce her risk of leukemia, help her improve her gait, help her speak clearly?"

"That's a different question altogether. That's a question of healing Lily, not preventing Lily."

"I confess, I'm not so interested in the healing of one person. I'm interested in the healing of humanity."

"To create a superior race?"

"I am not a Nazi, Annabel. I am a scientist, employing all the knowledge imparted to me to make the world a better place."

"The Nazis thought a world without Jews would be a better place, and a world without people with mental disabilities would be preferable."

"Yes, Annabel. I think you are right." Brad clears his throat and I hear him draw a long breath after. "I don't think ours would be an optimum working relationship. Actually I think it would be quite strained because I think, I'm pretty sure, you just compared me to Hitler."

"No, Brad. That's not what I'm saying. At all. I know you would never advocate killing anyone. I know you just want to help."

"Yes, that's what I'm aiming at here."

"I'm just saying be careful trying to build a Utopia."

"OK. I guess I'll take comparisons to Plato over Hitler."

"Actually, it was Sir Thomas More, who first coined the term, Utopia, in his book by the same name."

"Yes, but it was Plato who first had the idea of a perfect society. Remember *Plato's Republic*?"

"Yes, yes. Right you are. Again."

"I wish you all the best, Annabel. Really. I wish you much happiness. If indeed, happiness is the purpose of life."

めᏰɼᏰᏰɼᏰめᏰɼᏰめᏰɼᏰめᏰ

It's day four now of mail opening. It is well past noon. I had intended to try to get through the mail early each day, leaving time to write grant proposals for my next project. But the morning got away from me. I was looking through bridal magazines, trying to envision myself in all the wedding gowns, hearing Brad's voice appraising them, finding something not quite right about each one. I don't know why I listen. He is not the one I am marrying. Maybe the mail will bring better news. I find a letter postmarked Kingston.

Dear Annabel,

I wanted to let you know of a most amazing thing that happened here. Bennie has continued talking, so we were able to find out things about him we never knew. The other day, we tracked down his mother. She is a very old and poor woman, who lives in a cardboard shack and sleeps on the dirt floor. She has such horrible arthritis, she can barely sit up and would be dead if it wasn't for a neighbor bringing her an occasional meal every other day or so. But when she saw Bennie, her face lit up and she began to weep. He bent over her and hugged her, with a hug so tight, she nearly left the ground. We've brought her to the mission so we can care for her at the home for women. Bennie visits her every day, sometimes two or three times a day. He serves her at her table and sits and eats with her to keep her company. They smile at each other and laugh together, and sometimes they even have a conversation. She has told him she is sorry for abandoning him — that she didn't see any other way of keeping him alive than to leave him at the mission, but she cried for him every day of her life. He was able to tell her, in his own words, that he has never held anything against her and that he has had a good life and she should not feel guilty.

Someday, Annabel, maybe you can come visit us again and meet her. I'm sure she would enjoy meeting the person who was responsible for her reunion with her son. It has done a world of good for both of their souls, much more than I can go into in this letter.

Praying that God will continue to bless you abundantly,
Father Julian

P.S. Crazy Eddie says to tell you the rainbow bird has taken flight. He said you would know what that means.

I know what Marty will say.

"You see? It was all worth it," he will say. "It was all worth it."

෨❀ଓ

The Bird of All Colors

Marty's phone rang four times and then went to voicemail. I hung up. Ten seconds later, my phone rang.

"Hello, Marty."

"Annabel. So good to hear your voice. How are you?"

"I'm exhausted. But well. How are you?"

"Well. All is well. Why are you exhausted?"

"Up all night."

"Really?"

"Yeah, I couldn't sleep. Too much on my mind. Did you get a letter from Father Julian?"

"Yes. Incredible, huh?"

"Yes. Marty, I think I might be starting to believe in miracles."

"Told ya."

"I don't know how God does it. I don't know how He does what He does with the messes we make."

"He sees our good intentions."

"I'm not sure I had any of those. A reasonable person might assume I went to Jamaica to help, but I didn't."

"Why did you go?"

"To run away."

"Run away from what?"

"Questions. I want to go back again someday, Marty. This time for the right reason. I want to go for them, not for me."

"Me too. I'm going to try that next time too. If I can

manage to go again."

"What are you talking about? That *is* why you go."

"No, I've always gone for some need inside myself. There are countless rewards."

"I think we all need each other, Marty. It's impossible to give without getting something back."

"The paradox of self-sacrifice. You can never quite accomplish it. Trying to empty yourself, you get refilled all the fuller."

"Listen, I was wondering. You remember when you offered to write a song for my wedding?"

"Yeah? I remember."

"Well, I'd like to see what you can come up with."

"Really?" His voice lost its lilt here. "So you're getting married after all."

"I hope so."

"Well, I haven't done much writing since the accident. I'm not sure I can come up with something you will like."

"I'm sure I'll like it, Marty."

"I guess I can always get my buddy Chad to help. He's a good guitarist. And he's got a nice voice. You'll like him. He can play whatever I write. Sure, I'll give it a try if you need me to. Might be kind of fun."

"Yes, I would really like you to. I'll give you all the details when I see you. When can we get together?"

"Well, uh, I'm not really doing anything right now."

"Great. Do you want me to come over there or can you stomach the stacks of dirty dishes and piles of stinky socks of a woman who is insane from sleep deprivation?"

He lets out a brief chuckle. It's so good to hear him laugh. "You decide," he says.

"OK, I'll come over there."

Marty has a pile of books stacked on his coffee table, mostly fantasy fiction. *Two Towers* and *Frankenstein* lie open, face down. It occurs to me that Marty and I have never discussed literature.

"You a *Lord of the Rings* fan?"

"Yeah," he smiles.

"That makes sense."

"It does?"

"You are Frodo Baggins, if I ever knew one."

"Dang. I always thought I was Aragorn."

"I'm sure most men would aspire to be Aragorn. But he's not my favorite character."

"Actually, I think most men aspire to be Legolas. Something about that cool bow and arrow."

"If you ask me, you could be the entire fellowship rolled into one."

He laughs and offers me a cup of coffee. We move into the kitchen and sit at the table while it brews.

"So, did your friends, Dennis and Jimmy, get around to everything you needed done?"

"Yeah. They are good friends. To tell you the truth, I don't really need that much help, but they wanted to take care of everything. And that's good for them."

"Can I do anything, Marty? It would be good for me too."

"Well, yeah. You can answer some questions about this song you'd like me to write. How, again, did you and Brad meet?"

"Brad? Oh, I'm not marrying Brad. And I won't be working with him either. I'll probably never see him again, actually. Except maybe at some hors d'oeuvre table at some black-tie affair."

"That other guy then, the architect. Logan, right?"

"No, not Logan either."

"So, if you don't mind me asking, who are you marrying? I might want to, you know, work names into the song."

"No, I don't mind. Actually, I was hoping you would

ask. Though, I don't know how lyrical it will sound in a song. I'm not sure you can find anything to rhyme with "none of the above."

Marty squints and cocks his head slightly.

"So how about this?" I say. "How about 'Marty.' Does that work?"

He studies my face for several seconds, seemingly trying to determine what I just said, if he heard it correctly, if I really meant it and if he might be mistaken about my intent.

"Marty," he says finally. "Yes, Marty is a solid name for a wedding song. A really, really, rock-solid name. And lyrical."

We smile wide at each other from across the table, our entire future, euphoric and faceless, between us in that three-and-a-half-foot space.

"If you don't mind me asking," he says. "How did you come to this decision? About the name."

"Do you think it's the right decision?"

"Absolutely. Although I can't say that I am unbiased. I am kind of partial to the name."

"Yes, so now I guess the only question that remains is where can I find a guy named Marty who will marry me."

"I don't think you'll need to look too far."

"That's good. I have come a very long way already."

"And you're right where you're supposed to be."

"No." I stand up and move toward him, kneel beside him and wrap my arms around his waist. He holds me tight with his one arm. He puts his face flush on top of my head. Warm tears spill onto my hair. "This is where I am supposed to be," I whisper.

We stay in that space for quite a while, and then he takes my hand, slides off the chair and sits next to me on the vinyl floor. It is worn but clean, and I imagine it has been recently mopped by Dennis and Jimmy. We sit the closest we've ever sat together because up to this point we had the cushion of friendship between us, and now something bigger has pushed that aside.

"So what do you think about that idea for the song then?" I ask.

"I like it very much."

"I'm sensing you don't love it."

"I do love it." He puts his hand on my cheek and looks into my eyes.

"I'm sensing a 'but' here."

He sighs, props his elbow on his knee, and rubs his hand across his forehead several times. "In my life, I have not been afraid of many things. But I've been afraid to love you."

"Why?"

"I've been afraid to love anyone. But someone like you. How does a person do justice to loving someone like you?"

"Justice? No, justice is not our gig, Marty. In a just world, I would have the missing arm. Love has taken yours. If I had to rely on justice, I could be struck down for asking you for the rest of your life. I don't deserve it. But I am being bold here, I'm putting all my faith in love, and I'm letting you know that you're the one I want to walk through this world with."

"I hate to press my luck, but why don't you want to walk through the world with Logan or Brad?"

"Tough question. I could. I could walk through the world with either one of them and be perfectly content. At least for awhile. Until the black bird comes. I came to this realization: Logan and I have never been in the trenches. Nor have Brad and I. How would we survive it? Our lives together are built on all these wonderful things that keep us suspended on the surface of life. But how long do those things last? Besides, I get this warm, heavy feeling in my chest when I think of you, Marty. And all I can do is think about what it would be like to have you kiss me. To have you sing me to sleep, and in the morning, wrap me in a blanket as we sit propped against our headboard drinking coffee, listening to the birds, watching the leaves sway outside our window. It's like I opened the curtain for the first time in my life and let the sun in. I haven't been in the dark or anything. But it's been filtered light. And now, the sun's rays are shining in my window. Actual rays of warm, golden sun. And everything looks different in the light."

"I've seen it too when we're together. I know what you're talking about."

"It's not just when we're together. It's all the time. Together or apart, just the fact that there's someone in the world like you. That's what casts a new light on everything for me."

"I will tell you, I thought of spending the rest of my life with you the first time I saw you. Not love at first sight. Just a feeling that something was about to unfold. And I told myself how ridiculous that was."

"Why? Why was it ridiculous?"

"Well, first because you had just been proposed to by a pretty substantial guy at a very important event revolving around that pretty substantial guy, who happened to also be very handsome, from what I know of what women think is handsome, and pretty charming, from what I know about what women think is charming. So I kind of thought you might end up marrying him. And not some guy with an associate's degree, a $14.50 per hour job, an average face at best, an alcoholic father and a history of habitual lies buried somewhere in his past."

I shrug. "Call me crazy."

He smiles and pushes his glasses back to the place where they always fall down again. "You're crazy."

I can't believe he hasn't tried to kiss me yet, but I will not be the one to make that move. I have already made all the others. "You know what?" I say, getting to my feet. "Actually, right now, I'm hungry. Really hungry. I don't think I've eaten anything of substance in days."

He smiles and stands up. "Do you want me to make you something?"

"Let's see what you've got." I open the fridge.

Marty gets a couple of mugs from the cabinet for the coffee that finished brewing quite some time ago.

"Oh my word!" I say into the refrigerator. "It's positively cavernous in here. What have you been living on?"

Marty comes up from behind and squeezes me around the waist. I turn into his embrace, and a wave of warmth washes over us, despite the refrigerator door hanging open.

"I am crazy too, Annabel. I really am. At the risk of sounding like Patsy Cline, I am."

I back up into the fridge door, still locked in his embrace, and the door shuts behind me.

"I'll go pick something up," he says. He slightly loosens his hold, and we walk arm-in-arm back into the living room. "What do you feel hungry for?"

"No, no, that's OK. It's getting late, and I should go soon and get some rest. We have quite a lot of planning in front of us."

My eyes fall on a guitar propped on a stand near the front door. I hadn't noticed it before. "I thought you left your guitar in Kingston."

"I left the Yamaha there. I would never give up my Ibanez." He reaches out and grasps the neck, but doesn't pick it up. "This was my first guitar. A musician never gives up his first guitar. Even if he never plays it again."

"Which reminds me. I came here to talk about a wedding song."

Marty sighs, still grasping the guitar, still looking at it. "Well, Annabel. If there ever was a song that should be sung, it is the one in my heart for you. But I don't know how I'm going to be able to bring myself to sing a cappella in front of all those people."

"What about getting your friend to play while you sing?"

He grabs my hand. "No, I can't, Annabel. I'm sorry. I know that's wimpy of me."

"No, Marty. It's OK."

"I'm sorry."

"No, no. Don't be. It's OK." I squeeze his hand tighter. "Song or no song, you're still the craziest guy in the world."

"And that's a good thing?"

"That's a good thing."

He smiles and grabs me in tight to him.

"Some day, when you write the song," I say into the softness of his faded Jamaican flag T-shirt, "you can give me my own personal serenade."

"Actually, I already wrote it."

"The one you sang for me in Kingston."

"No. That's your song. I wrote another one for us."

"Really?" I look into his face. "Could I hear it?"

"I don't know if you'll like it. It's not your typical love song."

"That sort of makes sense," I say, putting my head back on his shoulder. "We are not your typical lovers."

He doesn't let go of me, and begins to sing. His voice cracks. My face is still buried in his shirt, so I can't read his face, and I don't know if he is nervous or swallowing back emotion.

> The sun rises on Kingston
> where the yellow bird flies
> and sings into the sunrise
> Even now, miles away
> I can hear the singing
>
> We lost so many things
> when the black bird flew
> unfurling sheets of sorrow
> Even now, miles away
> I can hear the crying
>
> Crazy Eddie told us
> doan koo, don't look, doan koo
> Your eyes will tun to dust
> Your eyes will tun to dust
> And so they did for me and you
>
> Then the rivers flowed
> And we saw the sun

stretched and pulled and spun
by pain and grief and the beautiful One
Yet, to us, unknown

It was there I found you
In the shadow of wings
The bird of all colors
casting its hue
That's where I found me
That's where I found you

The sun rises on Kingston
where the yellow bird flies
and sings into the sunrise
Even now, miles away
I can hear the singing

And the bird of all colors
flies there too
I know for sure she does
through the sorrow, beneath the sun
borne on the wind of the beautiful One

About the Author

Sherry Boas is author of highly-acclaimed fiction, including *Until Lily, Wherever Lily Goes* and *Life Entwined with Lily's.* She began her writing career in a hammock in a backyard woods in rural Massachusetts when she was eight years old, writing a "novel" about the crime-fighting abilities of her Cocker Spaniel. Fourteen years later, she would draw her first writer's paycheck for a very different kind of story when she landed a job at a newspaper in Arizona. She spent the next decade as a journalist, winning news awards, but her heart still belonged to fiction. So, after twelve years at home with her four adopted and highly inspiring children, she entered the ranks of contemporary novelists and enjoyed immediate success for her subtle, faith-based literature available from Caritas Press. Boas is also author of *Wing Tip* and *A Mother's Bouquet: Rosary Meditations for Moms.* Visit www.LilyTrilogy.com or CatholicWord.com.

Other fiction titles available from
Caritas Press / Catholic Word

  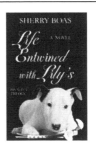
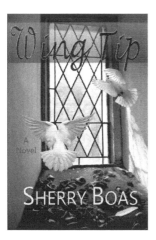

Rosary books from Caritas Press / Catholic Word

A Mother's Bouquet
Rosary Meditations
for Moms
by Sherry Boas

A Father's Heart
Rosary Meditations
for Dads
by Father Doug Lorig

A Servant's Heart
Rosary Meditations
for Altar Servers
by Peter Troiano

A Child's Treasure
Rosary Meditations
for Children
by Derek Rebello,
Elsa Schiavone &
Michael Boas

www.LilyTrilogy.com
or
www.CatholicWord.com

•

Made in the USA
San Bernardino, CA
30 May 2014